Cactus's Prick

J. Wine

This is a work of fiction. Names, characters, places, and events are products of the author's imagination or are used fictitiously. Any resemblance to actual persons, living or dead, or actual events is purely coincidental.

Cover design by Pretty In Ink Creations
Photograph by Volodymyr TVERDOK

ISBN: 979-8-9910220-4-0

CONTENTS

Disclaimers

This book is intended for readers 18 and older. It contains mature themes, strong language, violence, sexual content, and references to emotional and physical abuse.

Reader discretion is advised.

Chapter One

Why Did I Agree To This?

Roxy

"Did you fucking steal my money?" Jimmy screamed as he slammed the front door. "Goddamn it, Rox. Why didn't you pay the rent?"

"Roxy," I muttered under my breath. He couldn't see me from the living room, so I rolled my eyes as I flipped him off. It was time to put out another fire before he lit the whole place aflame. "Why do you always think I'm the one screwing you over?" I asked, walking into the living room. I sat next to him on the worn-out couch, making sure we weren't touching, in case I had to make a quick escape.

"The fucking landlord cornered me. He wanted to talk sports like we're friends. We're not, but he thought he was loosening me up before he asked about the rent. I told him I'd have to talk to you since it's your job to handle that shit. Did you fuck us over?"

"I paid the wife when I saw her the other day. She probably didn't tell him, but I got a receipt. Why the fuck do you always blame me?" I didn't ask the wife outright, but I was sure she had been stockpiling money to leave her husband. That was probably why the landlord didn't know I had already paid. If the landlord asked again, I'd show him the receipt as proof, covering our asses.

"Try not to do it again. You know how much I hate him. Thinks his shit doesn't stink." Jimmy's shoulders hunched as he sat on the edge of the couch, his elbows digging into his knees.

"He's better off than we are," I said. "Unless you want to buy an apartment building."

"Probably already knew you had paid, sick son of a bitch. Just wants what I have, knowing you take care of me. You're mine, so he should keep his eyes to himself," Jimmy said, turning on his video game.

My skin crawled. I hated the way those words slithered down my back, leaving a frozen trail of fear behind them. I was no man's possession, but it wasn't worth arguing about. Jimmy would push back, thinking it was a fight. It wasn't. He either didn't listen to what I said to him, or he simply didn't care. It could have been one or the other. At one point, I had thought this was going to be my forever, but each day I checked out a little more, not sure why I hadn't cut the cord.

"Some guy at work has been talking about loading his car and driving off. He didn't want to be tied down anymore, but the men on the crew laughed at him. Tried to sell us the idea of living free on the open road. Today, he finally did it. Shift ended, and the fucker drove off, his shit packed in the car." Jimmy's character died in the video game, and I couldn't help but think it was poetic justice.

"If you want a vacation, take a chair and stick it out in the back. That's about as much as our bank account can withstand."

Jimmy always believed his own bullshit, but it had taken me some time to see through the tall tales. We lived a few towns over from the Jersey Shore, so I didn't understand why he would want to go somewhere. If he really wanted a break from the monotony, we could lie on the beach for free.

I thought that was the end of the conversation, but the next night, he persisted.

"Come on, Rox. We'll hit the road. Free to go wherever the fuck we want." He cornered me against the kitchen sink. I never flinched anymore, preparing to handle whatever happened. "Think about it. We won't have to pay rent. No more living paycheck to paycheck. We'll actually have money for once. Be able to head wherever we want. Do whatever we want. I've never been over fifteen miles from the Shore."

I ignored the nickname, picturing the what-if. We were driving in a convertible on the open road, heading to our next destination. Real suitcases peeking out from the back, but we didn't own any. I'd have to pack our stuff using grocery bags. "How the fuck do you expect to pay for that? Ramen and vibes?" I crossed my arms over my chest, tiring of this conversation.

"You stop every now and again to work. Any restaurant is going to take you. Construction is a dime a dozen. When we stop, we'll stay a few weeks, see the sights, and then when we get bored, hit the road again. Come on, Rox. It'll be fun."

"No, thanks. If you want to go, I wish you the best." My mother had spent more money up her nose than she had worrying about her daughter. I'd grown up in poverty, and security was the only thing I craved.

"I can't do this without you. I don't want to, but you always shut me down. Don't you see I want to give you everything?" He laughed, kissing my lips before heading back into our tiny living room to play his game.

I've heard that one before. I swiped at my lips with the dishtowel, stretching my aching wrists.

The night after that, he pushed during dinner, when he'd normally complain that he hated whatever I had made.

A week later, I was lying on the couch, every bone in my body hurting. I had said nothing, but when I winced, Jimmy took me to the bedroom. For a second, I thought he might actually notice something besides himself. Instead, he made me lie on the bed, undressed me, and started to sweet-talk me. This was the first time he was offering pleasure.

"Don't stop," I begged, letting myself enjoy the attention. His fingers plucked my nipples while he used his other hand to bury two more deep within me. I'd experienced nothing like this, and I was so overwhelmed, I just lay there. My mind focused on each sensation, soaking it all in.

I was staring at the ceiling when I felt Jimmy bury his head between my legs. He licked my clit with abandon—something he'd never done before. "Please," I whimpered. I was so close to coming, and if he kept up the heavy strokes, I'd fall into oblivion.

Everything stopped as he picked up his head to ask me again. "Where would you want to go first? I was thinking about the Carolinas. There's plenty to do, and I heard they can't get enough people. Make enough to live like a fucking king."

As soon as he started talking, he snapped me out of the moment. I had to fake a moan, and he bought it, not knowing the difference.

He kept asking, and I kept saying no, until one night, the dinner service had nearly killed me. There had been a fight in the dining room over some guy's girlfriend going out with another man. They'd wailed on each other, running into tables, chairs, and other patrons. I had been in the wrong spot, holding a full tray, when one of them bumped into me. I couldn't move as the plates shattered around me. The heavy ceramic stabbed me in the legs. I prided myself on my service, but defeat overcame me that day.

Jimmy asked again as soon as I walked in the door. I smelled like diner food, there was probably glass stuck in the bottom of my shoes, and I needed a shower. I said yes. Not because I wanted to but because I had nothing left.

***

"When are you going to give it up, honey? Every man in here is dying for a taste. Some women, too," the head waitress said, dressed in a tube top and tight shorts. She thought she owned this place because her old man was an officer. Barked orders like the rest of us gave a shit.

"I have a boyfriend," I said, staring straight ahead. "Not interested, so there's more dick than you could ever handle floating around."

"If they want you, they'll find a way. Want to bet who gets some first?" Everything was a competition. I didn't have the heart to tell her I made more than she did in a night. The key was to keep enough covered to appear mysterious. A tight t-shirt and a pair of short shorts would do that.

It had been a year since we'd taken off from New Jersey, and this was my fifth biker bar. They were all the same. Different logos, same bullshit to worship. The brothers in this club were obnoxious. One night, they had a dick-measuring contest in the middle of the bar. Next, it was how many women they could bag. They used the nasty bathroom. I sure didn't give a fuck.

I kept their beers flowing and dodged any grabby hands. Tuning them out was the only way to survive. The only thing a biker bar was good for was quick employment. They didn't care if you vanished as long as there was no heat on the club.

"Girl! Jimmy's going to prospect. You'll have to roll the dice and see how many you can take. Your ass won't be so high and mighty then." She blew a bubble and popped it with her teeth in my face. "Better act nice. Depending on which brother you land, they might take it easier on you if you do."

Jimmy? Prospecting? It had to have been a joke. He'd never been interested before, so I wondered what had changed in the last couple of weeks. The club had its own rules and regulations, and Jimmy didn't have the discipline needed to be a brother. He had thought about it once, but when the club had handed him their code of conduct, that had been the end.

If this was his big plan to get ahead, we could have done that from home—New Jersey, not Williams, Arizona. Now, there was nowhere for me to run.

The bartender placed my bottles on the bar, popped the tops, and shoved them towards me. I had only a few seconds before I needed to move. Standing still meant unnecessary attention. Taking a deep breath, I smirked in her direction." I'm only here to make money until we move on. You're stuck here permanently. Good luck with that."

This was for the president and his buddies, and if I played my cards right, he'd leave a crisp one-hundred-dollar bill on the table. I could stomach the pig as long as the money was flowing my direction.

"Roxy." Ripper rolled my name off of his tongue as I sat his beer in front of him. "When are you going to keep me company? I'm bored."

I wanted to say never as I moved around the table, but I didn't know how he'd react. It was a toss-up between fight and flight. "I can't. You don't pay me to sit." It was the truth, so I didn't feel too bad about my retort. I pushed my luck, seeing if he would tell me anything more. "Besides, you have club girls for that, and Jimmy is not one of you."

The tables had plenty of space in between, which was one of the few reasons I stayed. As long as I kept my backside away from the table, no one could grab a handful. I could also see anyone coming before they snuck up on me. There were gropes and grabs all the time. Some waitresses even encouraged it, hoping for a bigger tip.

"Yeah, I've had all the rest." He picked at the label on the bottle. "It's not fun when it's the same old thing."

If he thought that was going to make me give in, he was sadly mistaken. In fact, I was thinking it was time to go. If Jimmy was really prospecting, he could stay here. I was fine hitting the road myself. I had too much self-respect to be passed around like a fucking rag doll, and they would.

"Jimmy's a piece a shit. He knows how it works around here but doesn't seem to care. Only a matter of time." He slugged the rest of his beer before letting out a loud belch.

"He's had other opportunities to prospect, but he has a hard time with the code of conduct." I could speak freely in the bar, but if I was overly harsh, someone would think it was their duty to discipline me. I'd already seen this happen to another waitress.

Ripper threw his head back and laughed. "Keep sweet. Once he wears the patch, you're mine. Jimmy's out right now with the enforcers learning the ropes." He swiped his tongue against his lips before flicking it at me. If that was supposed to excite me, it had the opposite effect.

He thought he had me cornered. All he had done was convince me to run.

Chapter Two

Goodbye, Jimmy!

Roxy

I burst into the motel room, beelining for the bathroom to collect my toiletries. I had never had enough money for luggage, and I wouldn't stop packing long enough to worry about it now. My mind raced, thoughts scrambling. I couldn't think.

My clothes went into as many grocery bags as I could find. I laid my change jar on top of the bags, opening and closing the dresser drawers until I found it—the tip money I had shaved off the top to hide. Jimmy never looked in the drawers, so they had been perfect when I thought I needed a nest egg.

Sitting on the bed, I asked myself if this was the right call. *Am I really going to throw two years down the drain?* Panic ensued. Jimmy had been good to me. Sure, there had been problems, but what relationship was perfect? For a second, I talked myself into pretending none of this was happening. *If Jimmy is prospecting, Ripper will get first dibs. They'll pass me around.* It wouldn't matter. I'd never escape that personal brand of hell.

Grabbing my things, I let the motel door slam behind me. I couldn't take the chance of being wrong. The stakes were too high for me, even though Jimmy had been the one to create this mess.

Slamming the trunk down on my car, I was ready to take off—with or without him. I was sitting in the driver's seat with the doors locked when I finally took a minute to breathe. I closed my eyes, trying not to feel guilty. *What if I'm wrong?* Jimmy was no saint, but it could have been worse.

Suddenly, I heard screams, but I couldn't find the source. Sitting forward in my seat, I surveyed the rows of motel doors for any sign of distress.

"Don't touch me," I heard a woman scream. "Help me!"

It went silent. I didn't have a plan, but I wanted to help her. I just couldn't find which room she was in.

"Please. Please don't hurt me." *That could be me—screaming behind a closed motel door, hoping someone would save me.*

Turning the key, my car started, and yet, I still hesitated. The screams continued, but I was too paralyzed to move. A truck pulled into the lot, and I recognized some enforcers from the club. Stopping right in front of my car, the back door opened. Jimmy jumped out of the truck, wearing a club cut. Every doubt I'd buried hit me like a gut punch. I had to get out. Now.

He knocked on my window as the rest of the men watched. I rolled it down just enough so he could hear me. "What are you doing?" he asked. He spoke with measured words. I had never heard him like this. "What the fuck are you doing?"

"I know how you get when the gas is low...I forgot to stop. I figured I'd go fill it before showering." It sounded plausible, but I needed him to buy it.

He made a humph sound and waved the men off. "They thought you were running, but you'd never do that to me. You're mine."

"No." It barely scraped past my throat. He had said it before, but this time, he meant it. He believed he owned me.

"Hang on a sec," he said, walking around the car to the passenger door. I didn't have a choice but to unlock it. "I'm hungry," he said, sitting in the passenger seat.

The drive to the gas station was heavy. It wasn't far, but each turn felt excruciating. Left. Right. The air in the car was suffocating as neither of us said anything. I nearly breathed a sigh of relief when I turned into the lot, finding an empty pump.

Jimmy opened the door, heading for the convenience store. He hadn't given me money for gas, and that was another strike. He'd stopped paying for daily expenses, claiming he couldn't find work. I had kept us afloat, and now, it was obvious I would pay with my body to give him the lavish lifestyle he craved.

I observed as he opened the door, not bothering to hold it for an older tourist. His head bobbed over the aisles, and I watched as he grabbed a few things. He hadn't asked whether I wanted anything.

I hadn't turned the car off. I didn't think as I put it into gear, driving off into the sunrise.

Goodbye, Jimmy. You chose this.

***

I kept checking my rearview mirror for motorcycles. No one followed, but that didn't ease my anxiety. It wouldn't take much for Jimmy to alert the club that I was missing.

Putting miles between me and them, I wasn't sure where I was going. I didn't think Flagstaff was far enough. I stopped to get some sleep in Phoenix. The city seemed too large, so I kept moving once I felt refreshed. Tucson was too dirty. I didn't know where I would end up, but when an exit sign appeared, I didn't hesitate. I was tired of the highway, but the scenery was pretty. That was all I cared about, for now.

I let the road guide me, listening to whatever country station came in through the radio. I was singing along with a man who'd lost his girl when I heard it.

Thump.

I had seen nothing in the road, so I ignored it, singing loudly again.

Thump. Kerplunk.

Yup, I had a flat tire in the middle of the desert.

I pulled onto the shoulder and sat in the blast of air conditioning. It was hotter than Satan's ball sack, and I wasn't enthusiastic about sweating my ass off while changing the tire. At least I was doing something for myself. If Jimmy were here, he'd be standing over me, yelling at how slow I was going.

I was just about to close my eyes when smoke rose from under the hood. *More shit I don't fucking need.* Quickly turning the car off, I sent up a prayer that once this was over, the car would start again, and I'd be on my way. This was just a minor inconvenience, or so I told myself.

The tire was the easier of the two, but I thought twice as I opened my car door. The desert sun hit me square in the face as I stepped around to the trunk. Moving all of my shit to the back seat, sweat soaked my tank top, but the tire wouldn't change itself. Grabbing the wrench and the jack, I was determined to save myself and get the fuck out of here.

It didn't escape my attention that I was the only living soul. No truckers—not even a lost car—passed me. I wasn't afraid, but I was smart enough to know I needed to move quick.

A humming noise surrounded me. The land was so barren that the sound bounced off the mountains in the distance. It was coming closer, each beat matching my pounding heart. I didn't want to admit it was a motorcycle as I crouched in front of the tire, wrench in hand. I tried to work faster, but nothing seemed to go my way. My legs shook as cramps settled in. A motorcycle zoomed past me, and I breathed a sigh of relief. I didn't want them to think I needed their help. I'd do this myself, even if it took all night.

I heard the motorcycle again. This time I turned my head toward the sound, hoping I was wrong. Dust kicked up in the distance, and my chest tightened again. He was coming back. Alone, with no one watching, I'd forgotten what it was like to be a woman. I went back to the nuts, keeping my ears pinned to the sound, listening as it rapidly approached me.

A man's voice rang out as he killed the engine. "There are coyotes in these parts. Are you planning on asking for help or waiting to be bait? Animal or man, it doesn't matter."

"Don't need your help," I said, keeping my eyes on the nut, like loosening it would unravel me. I figured if I kept my head down and didn't give the biker a sign I gave a shit, he would lose interest and go away.

"I didn't offer." His voice was wary, as if he thought there was more to this situation than there was. I had popped a tire, and if I wanted to get going, it was going to need to be changed. That was it.

"Of course, you didn't. A biker rolls up and assumes he's the white knight," I muttered, but when the biker groaned, my head shot up. He'd parked his bike behind my car, but he still sat on the seat, feet planted in the dirt. I watched as he pulled the bandana away from his face and let it hang around his neck. Dirt streaks covered his forehead, and there was an obvious line between where the bandana had sat and the bottom of the sunglasses he wore.

"So you're the obstinate princess. Got it. Doesn't make me want to help you any better," he said, unclipping his helmet from underneath his chin. The veins in his arms stood out, all strength and power.

Been here, done this. It only made you run.

"I could get that changed for you."

He's just a biker. Don't be a sucker for a bad boy, Roxy.

I went back to work on the lug nuts, but as I cranked the wrench, it slipped, smacking my knuckles. "Ouch!" I cradled my injured hand to my chest. I bit back a scream, tasting blood. Pain wasn't new, but I'd forgotten I had an audience until he exhaled through his nose. I lurched upright too fast. My legs gave out, dumping me into the dirt, slamming my hand against the ground. The pain radiated up my arm.

"If you'd just asked me nicely, I could have been done by now."

"Who says I'm not already regretting every minute of this?"

"Fuck this shit," he said, throwing his leg over his bike. He approached me with measured steps, one foot in front of the other. I tried to look away, but my eyes constantly calculated how close he was. My pulse picked up with each measurement.

I didn't see his club cut until he came closer—the one-percent patch sending a chill down my spine. My stomach knotted. I'd just left a one-percent club, and here was another. *Is this going to be a common thing?* I knew enough. He wasn't a man to play with, and I couldn't run. He'd probably give chase.

He leaned against the trunk of my car, crossing his arms over his chest, hiding the patch from my view. I wasn't sure if he had done it for me, or if this was his natural stance. I wasn't about to ask, letting on that I knew what the patch represented. His brows furrowed.

"I don't get it. What the fuck is going through your head?" His hand came up, waving around, as if I didn't know we were in the middle of the desert. "Last chance, sweetheart," he said, jaw tight. He shoved his sunglasses up and rubbed his eyes.

"I'm fine," I said. "You don't have to stay." My voice shook, but I was hoping he hadn't heard it.

"What are you so afraid of that you won't ask for help?" I should never have taken my eyes off of him. He moved quicker than I could react, grabbing the wrench from my hand. I quickly stood as he stalked past, yanking open the back passenger door and pointing at the seat. "Sit."

My brain screamed, but my body froze as I stared at him. It always remembered first. He was very close to the car. I wouldn't put myself in the position of being cornered. I had visions of being knocked out with the wrench. He'd shove me in the car, and I wouldn't have anyone who would know to look for me.

He took a few steps away from the door. We shifted around each other until I was closer to the seat, and he crouched down, sighing as he analyzed my blown tire. He finished removing the lug nuts in quick succession, and it was obvious this wasn't his first time. It would have taken me all night, but he made it look easy.

He stood, dusting his hands on his pants before pulling the tire off of the hub. I leaned forward, my gaze following him as he rolled it towards the trunk. It wasn't like he could go through my things. The bags were behind me in the back seat, untouchable without a fight. If I could get out of here quicker, I wouldn't complain. He didn't ask me for help, barely saying anything as he raised the trunk lid. When he reached for the spare, I saw only his arm as he jerked it out. It bounced to the ground before he set the flat down. He was a biker, and they took what they wanted without bothering to ask for permission. I understood, but I was safer if he ignored me.

Grabbing the spare, he rolled it back into position. I was silently counting down until this was over, but he stopped to examine the tire, and I had to crack my knuckles to release the pressure. He trapped the tire between his legs, placing his hands on either side. Every so often, he would flip it, stopping to look at the tread before rotating the tire again.

"You know this tire is bald, right?" He focused on me, waiting for a response.

I shrugged, knowing what he was asking me and not having an answer.

"Sweetheart," he snapped. "Pay attention. If this doesn't pop, you'll probably get to Tombstone, but not much past that." He swiped at the sweat on his forehead with his sleeve. "Where are you heading?"

"Why?" I said too quickly. I didn't want him to follow me. I didn't care if he thought he was making sure I was safe. There was no way I could outrun him in my car. I couldn't think fast enough to come up with a plan. "So you can stalk me later?" I cringed when I heard what I had said. No stalker was going to tell the truth, and now I'd alerted him to my line of thought. "No, thanks."

"Yeah, like I don't have other...better things to be doing," he deadpanned, placing the first lug nut back on.

I'd just left a man who hadn't respected me. I didn't need to encourage another one in the middle of the desert. Especially a man who appeared old enough to be my daddy. I should have kept quiet, but the words were already out of my mouth. "I'm not a damsel in distress." Saving face was more important in those few seconds.

"I need you to pop the hood." He clapped his hands, the dirt floating through the air as he ignored what I had said.

"Excuse me? I'm not popping out a boob."

"Didn't ask to see a boob. Have you looked at yourself lately?" He raised an eyebrow in my direction, probably regretting stopping. "If you're going to survive this trip, you need to pay attention. I saw smoke when I first passed you." He stood, throwing the wrench and the tire into my trunk before shutting it. "If you want to pop something else, that's on you."

I didn't know what he was talking about, but I caught my reflection in the window as I stood, shutting the door. "Dry heat, my ass," I groaned. My tank top was white, and it stuck to my bra. He didn't have to ask to see. He could have just looked anytime he wanted. There wasn't much left to the imagination, and I felt like a fool. "Not interested," I called out behind me. *I'm not popping anything for him.*

All I wanted to do was grab a crappy motel room for the night and start looking for a job tomorrow. The car was going to need some maintenance, but I didn't mind, as long as it got me out of here. Some gut feeling told me to leave. I didn't have an outstanding track record with one-percenters, and while he hadn't made a move to hurt me, I didn't want to take any chances. My gut was screaming at me to drive, and I was a firm believer in its mystical powers. As long as I was far away from here, I'd figure it all out later.

Sitting in the driver's seat, I started the car, praying the engine would turn over. It sputtered, but wouldn't start. Leaning against the headrest, I closed my eyes. Saying a quick prayer, I turned the key again, desperate for the engine to turn over. It sputtered and then stopped. "Come on, baby," I whispered, hoping the sweet-talking would work. The engine puttered and then gave up. My thumb rubbed the vinyl of the steering wheel. "Come on, baby," I tried again, but I didn't have any hope.

Third time was the charm. The engine purred as if there had never been an issue. I'd never been lucky, but I couldn't believe my good fortune. A dry chuckle escaped my lips as I put the car in gear.

I didn't think twice as I took off. The tires kicked up rocks in his direction.

I fought the urge to look in the rearview mirror. I had been in the wrong, but it wouldn't be a problem . As soon as I was far enough away, I'd put this all behind me—never seeing him again.

Chapter Three

Welcome To Tombstone

Roxy

There was a knock on my window.

I didn't recognize the sound at first, but I'd been jumping at every little thing the whole night, and I figured this was just more of the same. Burying myself further under the blanket, I squeezed my eyes shut, willing myself back to sleep. *Just a few more minutes.*

There was another knock on the window, a little louder than the first.

"Fuck off," I grumbled, rolling as best I could to face the back seats.

"You can't park here."

"Fuck." Flipping the blanket off, I sat up. Yawning, I rubbed my eyes, but the person outside was impatient. They knocked on my window again. "If you break it, you bought it," I exclaimed, putting my shoes on. I didn't bother with anything else as I flipped the door lock, the heat hitting me in the face as I got out. "What's your fucking problem?"

"Do you know where you are?"

I blinked twice until she came into focus, and then I had to blink a few more times to make sure she was real. She was a stunning brunette, oozing confidence I would never have. "Tombstone," I answered.

"At least that's something. You're sleeping in the main street's visitor's lot, and if the sheriff comes by, he'll tow you."

"I'm visiting." It was the first thing I could think of to get myself out of this situation.

She threw her head back and laughed. "Keep telling yourself that. This place has a funny way of keeping people." She surveyed me from head to toe, but when she found what she was looking for, she crooked her finger. "Come with me."

Grabbing my keys, I locked the car, not sure why I was blindly following. Dressed in a crisp polo with a logo and a denim skirt, she reeked of sophistication, but there was something that told me not to fuck with her. I was comfortable in my skin, but walking behind her, it was clear who was in charge as she led me out of the parking lot.

The minute we stepped onto the sidewalk, I felt like I had transported back in time. They had roped off the street from regular traffic, and I walked out to stand in the middle. It was early morning, and there wasn't much activity, but it wasn't hard to imagine what this place would have looked like in its prime.

"I've seen that look before," she said, coming to stand next to me. "It's technically a small town, so you relish the quaintness, the charming atmosphere of it all, not realizing you're being sucked in, until it's too late."

"I'm just visiting," I reminded her. Once I had the car fixed, I'd do a few touristy things to remember the place and then hit the road. I had gotten used to the travel, and it wasn't bad when you had nothing else waiting for you.

She made a noise, like she didn't quite believe me. "At this end of the street are the new businesses, mostly. Trinket shops for the tourists, that kind of thing. In the middle are the saloons and restaurants, and the far side is the historical. Before you leave, take a tour through the museum and see the show. It's always fun the first time." She continued walking down the dirt street.

My head was on a swivel as I followed her, trying to take it all in. I didn't know what time it was, but there were shopkeepers outside, propping up chalkboard signs and sweeping the boardwalk. If they looked up and saw us, they waved and called out a greeting. I wasn't sure if this was a close-knit community, or if she just wielded that kind of power. Turning towards the Blue Angel Saloon, she opened the front door, letting me stand in the entranceway.

I didn't know what I was expecting, but this wasn't it. I was having a hard time merging the past with the present, and the saloon wasn't any different. There was a second floor with four doors, the railing running the length of the room. Anyone could stand and watch the dining room from that vantage point. If this were Nevada, I might have worried.

Kerosene lamps were everywhere to create an ambiance, but I doubted they were functional. I didn't look too closely, but there were outlets cleverly disguised on the walls. Heavy red brocade curtains draped the stage at the back of the room. I waited, not sure what I was supposed to be doing.

"This is your one chance," she said, lifting the gate and sliding behind the bar. "What were you really doing out there?"

"I need a job, and I thought I'd check to see who was hiring, but when I went to leave, the car wouldn't start. It was too late to call someone, so I stayed."

She shook her head as if this wasn't the first time she'd heard a similar story. "Grab a seat, and I'll make coffee."

I assumed she was the owner or the manager of this place as she moved with familiarity, giving me extra time to take everything in. My eyes bounced around the room, never settling on any one feature for long.

"What's your story?" she asked, placing two steaming coffee cups on the table nearest to me before sitting down.

"What's yours?" I asked, still standing in the doorway. I wasn't sure if I should run and ditch the car, but the coffee smelled delicious, and I desperately wanted a cup.

"It's safe." She nodded to the cup, waiting for me to sit down across from her before she pulled out her phone. Hitting a button, she placed it at her ear. "Morning, Sheriff. How are you?" She waited a minute before she chuckled. "You saw it, huh? It's my new girl, and she didn't know to park in the back. That's my fault, but now the car won't start." There was a pause before she continued.

"Don't worry, I'll call them, and we'll get it taken care of. If you're in the area, stop by, and I'll buy you lunch."

No sooner had the phone call ended than she hit another button. "Aces, I need a favor," she said, not bothering with the pleasantries. "I don't care, nor did I want to know there are two women tied to your bed." She rolled her eyes at me. "Car won't start, and my new girl parked it in the visitor's lot." She tapped her manicured nails on the table before picking up her coffee and taking a sip. "Do I need to call Scorp?" she asked, her smile turning up at the edges. "I thought so. We'll see you soon." She hit end and placed the phone on the table, facedown.

"You're lucky it was me who caught you out there. It's the twenty-first century, and yet this town has never moved forward. Every day is like a new game of cowboys and outlaws." She set her coffee cup on the table and extended her hand out to me. "I'm Angelica."

"Roxy," I said, shaking her hand. I took another sip of my coffee. "Why are you helping me?" No one had ever lent me a hand without wanting something in return. I couldn't even imagine what her request could be.

"I've always thought the best of people, but I stopped offering to help the last time I got burned pretty badly. You remind me of myself when I came to Tombstone, but that girl is long gone now." Angelica tilted her head to the side and shrugged her shoulders. "I'll get your new-hire paperwork in a few, but let me give you a quick rundown of the place. We open with the strip at nine, but once the regular businesses close at five, we serve dinner until nine."

"You didn't ask whether I have experience."

"You do. If I had to guess, you started at sixteen, and you've gone from one restaurant to another." She chuckled. "Plus, you had a pair of non-slip shoes lying on the floorboard in the back seat."

I chuckled, trying to hide my resentment as I took the last sip of my coffee. I wasn't running from anyone, nor was I in danger, but I didn't like being clocked so easily.

"This is a working saloon, and before you go, we'll fit you for a uniform. It's not bad, but most guests will be tourists who want an authentic experience. They'll gawk and make stupid jokes. Just stay away from grabby hands, and you'll be alright. If I see it, I put a stop to it, but men are sneaky."

I nodded my head, completely understanding. I'd spent more than my fair share working places I shouldn't have. Roadside diners, biker bars, and truly awful places—they all deserved to be burned down and forgotten. Dodging grabby hands wouldn't be a problem for me, but it should never have been an issue to begin with. I thought of the biker who'd stopped yesterday, proving my point.

"The regulars will remember your name. We have the best food on the street, and they don't have any other choice. They float in and out during the day, but most stick to themselves at the bar. We also make sure delivery orders are right, but there's nothing exciting about those. I'll give you the crash course after we've taken care of your car. You'll start tomorrow."

"What if I fuck up?" It was a distinct possibility, knowing my history. I had a bad habit of making slight mistakes that ended up turning into a huge clusterfuck. Once, I had been serving an enormous table in a cramped restaurant with hardly any space to maneuver with a tray. I had figured it wasn't a big deal, stacking the plates along my arms, and if it took two trips, so be it. I hadn't expected to walk through the dining room with my arms stretched out like a mummy.

As I had passed a table, the patron had accidentally bumped me, sending me tumbling to the floor. I had saved the food, but I had failed to notice I was standing on the tablecloth. When I had tried to move, my shoes yanked the cloth, pulling everything with it. Plates, glasses and silverware had come crashing down. Shattering glass had echoed across the room as the drinks poured over the edge, soaking my socks in a cold, sticky mess.

"You won't." A look passed between us, almost as if we had lived the same past. I asked no more questions, for fear she'd rescind the job when she realized I hadn't been joking. "Let's go get your stuff before the boys show up to take the car to the garage."

We walked back out onto the street before she stopped me.

"Welcome to Tombstone, Roxy."

Chapter Four

It's Not Free, Fucker

Cactus

"You're late," Scorpion said as I walked through the front door of the clubhouse, into the main room.

"It was a long night, and things didn't go as planned." I yawned, loosening the ache in my back from the ride. The last thing I wanted to do was deal with his shit. I had vouched for him when he prospected, even helped him keep his life together when he was about to be a father, not expecting a thank you. However, it had been hard not to hold a grudge when I'd gotten the call to settle back in Tombstone. He'd failed, and I had been the one to pick up the pieces. There were days I wanted to be back on the road, but I couldn't leave my family until Scorpion was trustworthy enough to protect them.

Every time I wanted to beat Scorpion to a pulp, I had to take a deep breath and remind myself I had chosen this life. I had taken the oath, burning it straight into my soul, but I walked a fine line when I had to deal with him. Respect came with the patch, even if I silently questioned every decision he made. He was my president, but I would never openly challenge him, despite our sullied past.

One of our best clients had called, swearing he was missing a piece of their shipment. If it had been anyone else, the club would have told him to go fuck himself, but we liked our bread buttered. Most of the brothers had come from broken homes where money was scarce. We didn't give a fuck what we had to do as long as the money was rolling in. I'd volunteered to take the ride out to buttfuck nowhere to handle it, but I hadn't expected a chick in the middle of nowhere with a flat tire.

"Seriously, did everything go all right?" he asked, leaning against the corner of the couch. I wondered when we would have to buy a new couch because his ass had imprinted on his seat.

"It was just a misunderstanding." I would tell him the whole story later, but that small piece was enough to calm his ass down for right now. He was a prick on a good day, but until he got properly laid, he'd be unbearable. Prick—the word made me think of the girl on the side of the road again. She'd been the reason I was late, but if she had damaged my bike when she peeled off like that, I would have had another emergency to deal with.

"Talk later than." He rubbed his eyes.

"If that was any good, you wouldn't be busting my balls," I said, pointing to the back of the blonde head between his legs. This was a typical morning in the clubhouse, and I was a little surprised there weren't more brothers getting laid in the main room. None of us cared who saw what, but her hair was so big, it completely covered his lap. "Dude, there's no sound. What the fuck is she even doing under there?"

"Who the fuck knows? There are two in Aces's bed, but he literally tied them up and locked the door when he got called out for a tow. Fucking freak." Scorpion shook his head, and I didn't bother to say anything, knowing he was right. If Aces had locked the door, he wasn't sharing them without an invitation.

"Sucks to fucking be you." I yawned again, plopping my ass in the chair next to him. I hadn't slept all night, preferring to make up for the time I'd lost changing the tire. *She owes me*, I thought, laying my head against the cushion and closing my eyes. *If I ever see her again, I'll get her to make it up to me—on her knees with a lot of tongue.* Groaning, I forgot where I was until Scorpion smacked his hand against my knee.

"If you want her to finish whatever that was, take her. My hand is better." He grabbed the back of her head, pulling her hair until she released him.

"I'm good," I said. I didn't have a problem taking sloppy seconds when they were actually good, but she would be more trouble than she was worth, which was why he was offering her to me. Scorpion would prefer that I be on the other end of whatever crazy she harbored.

Scorpion leaned forward, staring her straight in the eyes. "Get the fuck out of here. If I see you in my clubhouse again, I'll teach you how to give a proper blowjob, and you'll hate every minute." He wouldn't, but she didn't know that, running out the front door as tears streamed down her cheeks.

I was halfway through calling him an asshole when the front door to the clubhouse slammed, cutting me off.

"Dude, you need to control your Old Lady." Aces came storming into the room, Eights quietly following behind him.

"I don't have an Old Lady. Angelica's made it perfectly clear she wants nothing to do with my ass." Scorpion scoffed before interlocking his fingers behind his head. He'd severely fucked that up, and instead of making amends, he'd continued fucking everything in sight.

I shifted in my chair, making sure I could watch Scorpion. He would always swing first, not asking questions, whenever someone mentioned Angelica's name. Aces had already started the argument, but he never knew when to quit, and Angelica was clearly off limits.

"Your bitch called while I was busy, and when I told her no, she threatened to tell you. If she's not your Old Lady, she doesn't get those fucking privileges. Her new girl parked in the visitor's lot, and you know how the sheriff gets about that." Aces huffed, puffing his chest out.

"Not my bitch." Scorpion shifted forward, preparing to launch at Aces if he came close enough. It wouldn't matter that Scorpion's ass would be on display as his pants hung from his ankles. I slid to the edge of my seat, my hands resting on my knees, while Eights shifted to his toes, ready to grab Aces from behind if it came down to it.

"Where does she get these rejects?" Aces sighed, running a hand through his hair. "The girl's car wouldn't start, so it's currently sitting in the garage. I told Angelica I wasn't looking at it until tomorrow. I don't fucking work on an empty stomach or with a hard dick."

"Free lunch means we're fucking paying for it." Scorpion had bought the Blue Angel Saloon to win Angelica back, but she'd shut the door in his face—message received. They spoke only when necessary, or if it regarded their daughter.

"No, it means you're fucking paying for it." Aces flicked him off for good measure, deflating now that the fight was over. "You done?" he asked, pointing to Scorpion's dick.

"Didn't even start," Scorpion said, holding the waistband of his jeans as he stood.

"Come on. You can have the brunette." Aces headed towards his room, expecting Scorpion to follow him. "If you ruin my free lunch, I'm going to tell Angelica you only fuck blondes because brunettes remind you of her."

"I'm going to bed. Don't let me sleep past a free lunch tomorrow, since it's going on Scorpion's tab," I yelled after them before they turned into the hallway.

"It's not free, fucker."

***

Roxy

I had been eager but anxious to walk into the saloon for my first day. When I'd spoken to Angelica the day before, it had sounded like she was going to throw me to the wolves. While I knew I could do it, it would be a fight to prove I belonged, but Angelica had been right. Once the nerves settled, I was nailing my first day, which hadn't happened in a really long time. I smiled normally, but when I looked in the mirror, it was extra bright.

"I've known plenty of girls like you," she had said. "You don't want to let anyone in, but you'll turn on the charm to make a good tip. You have car repairs to pay for, and supposedly this is all temporary." She had laughed, her eyes sparkling as she shooed me out of her office.

She had made a few assumptions about me, but they had all been true. She didn't spew any bullshit, delivering the power punch under a cool veneer, and coming from someone like her, I wanted desperately to believe I could amount to her level of greatness.

No one had ever asked me what I wanted, but now that I was newly independent, I was planning on taking control of my life and dictating what happened to me. I wasn't someone who always found the negative, but it always seemed to find me, and I was tired. I wanted to break the cycle. Be confident in myself and my abilities. Angelica had proven it could be done.

I figured she had a past, but you would have never known it by the way she glided through the dining room. I still didn't know if she was the owner or just the manager, but she gave off the impression that you should thank her for allowing you into the saloon. Not the other way around. I'd watched her occasionally as she stopped at each table to introduce herself. She'd make small talk, ask them if they needed anything, and then move on to the next. She was almost too perfect to be real, and while I didn't aspire to that level of greatness, I wanted some of it to trickle down to me.

"You doing alright, honey?" the older waitress asked, waiting for me to look up from where I was pushing mashed potatoes into the trash. She was on her way out with a tray full of food, so I quickly nodded, letting her know I was fine. She'd been checking in with me for most of the morning, like the mother hen of the saloon.

Francene was past her prime, her gray hair in a pretty twist at the back of her head. I knew what it was like to run out of options, and when she had told me she only stayed because she had nowhere else to go, I could see myself doing the same thing. I wasn't sure where my journey was going to take me, but if I wanted to settle down, this was one of the nicest places I'd worked in. The corset with shorts they called a uniform sucked, but it could have always been worse.

Lulu sidled up to me as I finished. "Don't look now. The sexiest men alive just walked through the front door." She was almost as bad as a man. It didn't bother me, and most of the time I laughed as long as we weren't in the dining room. She was harmless but flighty, and I had a feeling that if I gave Lulu an inch, she'd try to take a mile, and I wasn't sure I had that kind of energy.

"They might be hot to look at, but no man is worth the trouble." I chuckled.

"If Aces wanted to tie me up, I'd let him." She smirked, bumping her hip into mine. "There's six of them, so I'll set two four-toppers up, but you should be alright to serve. We just won't give you another table until they're gone. You're welcome." She winked at me before sashaying out the kitchen door.

Washing my hands, I grabbed silverware before heading to the dining room. My smile was in place, but as I crossed the threshold, I froze. Sitting near the middle of the large table was the biker I'd left in the dust. Across from him was Aces, who'd taken my car to the garage yesterday for repairs. *Why the fuck does this shit always happen to me*? It had never crossed my mind that they knew each other.

My stomach dropped as more realizations came flying at me. Angelica had called Aces. She might not have been part of their club, but she was comfortable enough calling them for help. *Should I run*? Fear clouded my judgement, but I didn't want anyone to see weakness. They'd never let me live it down—I'd learned that from experience.

I plastered a fake smile on my face and forced my feet to move until I reached the biker sitting at the end closest to me. He was bald, with the bluest eyes I'd ever seen buried beneath wire-rimmed glasses. I didn't know his name, but he was reading the menu as I approached. If I wanted to keep my distance, he seemed like the safest bet.

Taking a quick breath, I introduced myself. "Hello, I'm Roxy, and I'll be your waitress for lunch." I smiled, giving myself an imaginary pat on the back. So far, so good, I thought as I started placing the silverware on the tables at their elbows.

"Be nice. She's new." Lulu winked at me as she ran past, running food towards the front of the dining room.

"She spits rocks pretty well," the biker from the side of the road commented drily. Our eyes met across the table. "Don't ya, Roxy?" he asked, raising an eyebrow.

"Only at men old enough to be my daddy." I didn't know why that was the first thing that popped into my mind. The table went silent, and even if they got me fired, it would have been worth it just to see the stunned expression on his face.

The man at the far end with the dark, shoulder-length hair laughed, and everyone else followed suit. "I like her," he said.

"You would, Scorp. Lay off." Angelica appeared, standing next to the bald-headed biker. She placed her hand on the back of his chair, confirming she was comfortable with them. "Lulu's right. Be nice to this one. We're trying to keep her."

"She's temporary. Right, Rox?" I could feel the tire changer's eyes following me as I moved around the table, but when he called me Rox, I stopped.

"Ro-xy," I corrected automatically. "Someone needs to sew your names into your club cuts. No one wants to be mistaken for Prick." I let the insult roll off my tongue, returning his gaze. Neither of us looked away as another round of laughter floated around the table. If I was getting fired, I was going out with a bang.

"Roxy." He smirked. His handlebar mustache twitched at the ends, but I thought it was weird when he stroked his pointed beard.

I quickly worked the rest of the table, and when I stood next to Angelica, I asked if I could bring them something to drink. They rattled off beers in no particular order, and I wanted to tell them they'd have to do better if they were trying to test me. I made an excuse, saying I'd be back to take their food order, before heading towards the register furthest from them. I needed a minute to calm down.

Angelica stepped up next to me. "How do you know Cactus?" she whispered.

"That's his name?" I swiped at one of my bangs, not surprised. "I had car trouble on the way here, and he stopped to help." While nothing had happened when he'd changed my tire, I didn't want to be involved in a lover's quarrel.

"He did what?" Her mouth puckered as if she couldn't believe what I was telling her.

"He stopped and changed my tire, but I took off before he could look under the hood. I wasn't about to become a statistic in the middle of the desert." I tried to explain as best as I could without jeopardizing my job.

"I would have, too." She laughed. "The daddy comment was priceless, though."

"Thanks, but I'll do better. It slipped off my tongue a little too easily, but I don't want any trouble." I had just dumped trouble off at a gas station in Williams, and this was supposed to be the relaxation period before I made huge life decisions. I side-stepped her, heading to the bar, but she stopped me, reaching out to grab my arm.

"If it were anyone else but those assholes, I'd care. Try not to make a habit of engaging with them, or they'll never stop." She smiled, but it didn't reach her eyes as she walked away.

Angelica didn't give me enough time to reassure her. I'd been around enough motorcycle clubs on this trip that I was well aware they were all the same. The men acted like Neanderthals, and the women were supposed to be grateful for the attention. No, thanks. I wouldn't have a problem walking away when my time here was done. At least, that was what I kept telling myself when Cactus's eyes burned holes into my back as I moved from the register to the bar.

Chapter Five

Hello, Cactus.

Cactus

I smirked, shifting in my chair as I watched her hips sway, each step evenly measured as she headed toward the furthest register. I suspected she wanted to run out the front door, never looking back. If she'd slipped, we would have torn her apart emotionally. No hesitation. We were assholes like that, but she held her own. It made me wonder where she'd been. What she had seen.

When I lost sight of her, I turned back around. We were here for a free lunch, but the dining room was full for a weekday. No one wanted to be out in this heat, and summer was traditionally slow.

"Is that the reason you were late?" Scorpion leaned forward in his chair, staring at me.

"What the fuck are you talking about?" Aces pointed his finger at Scorpion before shifting it to me, and then back to Scorp. "Eights and I towed her car."

Huckleberry, our enforcer, grinned. "They know each other. Weren't any of you paying attention when he called her Rox? There's some tension there, probably more anger though than sexual. Both are good. Gets the blood pumping to your dick." He would know, considering all the love bombing he did. We tried to tell him it wasn't necessary when you rode a bike and wore a club cut, but the dude didn't listen. He'd bat his blue eyes, and rub his bald head as if he didn't know what he was doing, and it worked every time.

I ignored them, sitting back in my chair to wait for my beer.

"I was waiting for her to rip your dick off and feed it to you, Daddy." Flash was laughing so hard he snorted. He'd probably journal this conversation later, rereading it over and over, until something else held his attention. When we'd nominated him for club secretary, he'd initially told us no, but then he'd pulled a pen from his pocket.

"Do I look stupid to you?" I asked Flash, not bothering to wait for an answer. "Found her on the side of the road, trying to get the lug nuts off the tire. It would have taken her most of the night, so I stopped, moving her ass out of the way. It's cute she thinks she can throw a tantrum, but it would have been stupid if she'd chipped my bike when she pulled off the side of the road. When she settles down and learns how to handle new toys, then I'll think about letting her thank me properly."

"I only play well with people my age."

She'd heard us. Starting with Huckleberry at the end of the table, she went around, laying the correct bottle next to the right brother. We'd rattled off our normal orders quickly to test her, and she'd passed with flying colors.

I felt her brush up against my shoulder, laying my bottle towards the middle of the table. None of the other brothers had gotten that treatment, just me.

"You know, so you don't accidentally spill it in your old age. We don't have bibs," she whispered.

My mouth dropped open as the rest of the brothers died laughing, but she moved on, like it was no big deal. My jaw was tight as I tried to come up with a winning retort. I was going to have to be quicker than that if I was going to one-up her, and I always won.

"With an attitude like that, it'd be real pretty to watch her submit." Aces's eyes rolled back into his head, and my knuckles itched to knock his fucking ass out. I stayed put, flexing my hands into fists underneath the table. This wasn't my fight.

Lulu heard him as she ran towards the kitchen. He hadn't even finished the sentence before she smacked him in the back of the shoulder. "There are plenty of willing prospects if you would just ask. Roxy would eat you up and spit you back out."

"Like you?" He turned in his chair, scanning her from head to toe. "You wouldn't last fifteen minutes in my bed."

Francene called out from behind the bar, getting Lulu's attention. I wasn't surprised she had a thing for Aces, but he'd never given her the time of day. Our executive team had agreed when Scorpion had bought this place. We didn't shit where we ate. There were plenty of prospects on this street if you knew where to look. Redheads? Check the museum. Ravens? There were a few at the stunt show in the middle of the strip. Blondes? They were a dime a dozen.

I held the rim of my beer bottle against my lips, preparing for the perfect taste, when it hit me. *Fuck.* As long as Roxy worked here, she'd be off limits. I raised my eyebrows, contemplating my next move as the beer slid down my tongue. However, the more I thought about it, the more Lulu was probably right. Roxy gave off man-eater vibes, and I liked my dick where it was.

Comfortable silence settled around the table as we listened in on the conversations floating around us. Someone always talked about something they shouldn't. One time, a kid was chatting with an older man about all the money he was going to spend on his baby mama after their delivery. Too bad they'd forgotten to mention it to us. By the time we took our cut of the profit, there wasn't anything left.

It wasn't much longer when Roxy appeared, carrying stacked plates up her arm. "Chicken sandwich," she said, laying the plate in her left hand in front of Eights. Walking around the table, she stood behind Huckleberry. "Cheeseburger with fries. I'll grab you ketchup in a second," she said, laying his plate in front of him with her right hand. Roxy had spent plenty of time serving, and that made me mad.

She worked the table like a pro, dropping plates left and right, and I wasn't the only one who noticed. Scorpion was paying attention, and each time she set a new plate down, his eyes narrowed. He was suspicious. As Sergeant at Arms, I was going to have to tail her to make sure she wasn't here for us.

"Steak and eggs. Do you need sauce?" she asked Scorpion, laying his plate in front of him. He reached out and grabbed her wrist. She squeaked, but I didn't think she was in pain, more surprised than anything else. "Let me go," she said evenly.

"What's your story? If you're here to hurt Ang, I'll just make you disappear right now, and we can forget about fixing your shitty car." His dark eyes stared at her, his fingers flexing around her wrist.

My ass was stuck to the chair. Scorpion was unpredictable, and I didn't need him to cause a scene in the saloon. There were too many people eating, and while we didn't care they knew we had an affiliation, we didn't need to show them how brutal we could be.

Roxy had earned herself a place on his watchlist. He didn't trust her, and I didn't need her picking up another admirer until I figured out her story. She hunched over the table, but his broad back hid his grip on her wrist, making the situation appear innocent. It was anything but.

"If you don't let me go, I'll stick your steak knife through your hand. I know the cops won't help me—I'm not that stupid—but you'll be very uncomfortable until my car is ready."

"I won't ask you again. What's your story? No one carries plates like that unless they've been waitressing since the Dark Ages. You're not old enough." His lip curled as he sneered at her.

"Temporary." She moved quicker than any of us expected. Grabbing his steak knife with her other hand, she went to stab him. He let her go just in time, but she was already driving the knife downward. Scorpion laid his hand flat against the pine table, but she drove the knife in between his splayed fingers. The handle stuck straight out of the wood. "You shouldn't have bet against me." Picking up her head, she smiled at the rest of us, almost too sweet. "Who would like a refill?"

***

Roxy

I met each biker's eyes, not willing to back down. "Beers?" I pushed, trying to get one of these fuckers to answer so I could leave the table. I added a smile, pretending there wasn't a steak knife sticking straight up out of it. A few raised their hands, as if this were a classroom. "Great. Enjoy your lunch, and I'll grab ketchup."

"Can I get a bottle, too?" This one is empty." The man sitting at the table behind Cactus shook the ketchup bottle as if I needed a demonstration. I'd seen him walk into the dining room with his wife and two boys, but since I wasn't waiting on them, I hadn't paid too much attention. Taking the empty with me, I told him I'd bring another. This was a simple ask, and I didn't mind pitching in.

Cactus's eyes followed me as I crossed the room to the bar, keeping my head high. I wouldn't do anything about it. This was a job, and for once, I was taking someone else's advice. I wouldn't entertain them. They probably had a million other women who would cater to their every need. I was getting tipped to serve them. It wasn't the same.

Placing their refill order, I grabbed two bottles of ketchup, delivering the first one to the father. The other one went to the biker at the end of the table with the bald head and blue eyes. "Here you go," I said, syrupy sweet.

"Thanks, darling." He winked at me. "You know, if you're—"

"No, thanks." I pointed at my name badge, pinned to the corset. "Temporary, remember?" I gave him a wink in return and pivoted on my heel towards the bar. The bottles were at the end, waiting for me. I clutched three in one hand and reached for Cactus's with my other. To anyone else, this might have been awkward, but not me.

You just have to survive another twenty minutes. Thirty tops. Just think—big tip. Huge.

I walked around the table, standing behind Cactus, but before I could lay his bottle on the wood, Aces started talking to me.

"Ro-xy." He smirked, his lips twitching, as his finger pointed at me, then Cactus, and back again.

I ignored him, brushing Cactus's arm as I set his beer on the table, in a reasonable spot this time. I wasn't playing around with them anymore, but that was when I felt it. The man for whom I had brought the ketchup had his hand on the back of my upper thigh—just beneath the hem of the shorts.

"I mean, if you're not interested in an old man like him, I'd sacrifice my dick. You know, for the greater good of humanity?"

Aces was still working his angle, but I froze. My skin crawled as my stomach lurched, threatening to vomit all over their table.

"Hey, I meant nothing by it. Well, I did, but you're looking a little pasty, and my dick shriveled. He likes to be only where he's wanted." Aces leaned forward in his chair.

My grip tightened around the neck of the bottle until I thought it would break in my hand.

Cactus turned in his chair, brushing against my arm that held the other three. My mouth opened to speak, but the words were stuck at the back of my throat. He hit my arm with his shoulder. The bottles tipped forward. The beer spilled down his back.

"What the fuck!" he yelled, and that was when I finally woke up. I jumped backwards, but all it did was give the man behind me a better grip as the bottles hit the floor. His grip was so tight that I couldn't move as the glass shattered. Thank fuck no one was filming this shitshow.

"What the fuck is wrong with you?" Cactus roared even louder, jumping from his seat. The glass crunched underneath his boots as the beer ran off the back of his club cut.

I could have told him it was his fault that he had bumped me, but I didn't know how he would react. It was easier if he let out the brunt of his anger on me. The only thing I wouldn't tell him was the truth. The man's wife had excused herself to the restroom, but the boys were still at the table. I didn't need them to be subjected to violence because their father was a creep.

I'd thought I could survive the first day. I was wrong.

Chapter Six

Stiffed on the Tip

Cactus

"Why do you constantly take in strays, Ang? Haven't you learned yet? They're only out for themselves," I yelled at her. She'd come running when she'd heard the breaking glass, ushering me into her office to dry off. My club cut hung from one of the office chairs, but the beer seeped into the leather pores. I was going to have to figure out how to dry-clean it without taking it to a professional. "If she can't keep her shit together, she's a liability. I'll have Aces fix her car, and she can be gone in a few days."

Ang didn't understand that this wasn't about the beer. It was about Roxy's reaction in the heat of the moment. She'd frozen. If that was her first instinct, she'd have more accidents the saloon would be responsible for.

"That's rude. You always jump to the wrong conclusion," she said, throwing a towel at my chest.

"How much do you know about her?" I pushed. This wasn't the first time Ang had tried to save someone, but she'd honestly be better off if Roxy didn't show up for her next shift. I wasn't the only one to think so, which was why Scorpion hadn't barged back here. He was busy watching Roxy's every move.

"I know enough." Ang crossed her arms over her chest, sticking her hip out. "You only see the negative in people, which is why you're still pretending to be big and bad at your age."

"You saw her. She couldn't even last one shift. What if she had bumped into something? Or what if it had been a kid trying to get her attention?" I dropped my shirt on the tiled floor, picked up the towel and rubbed it against me. "Do you really want to lose everything you've worked for? You exposed the saloon the last time you tried this."

"You've always been the protector, and if you hadn't been busy maintaining your image, you would have noticed the moment she froze. I know you. You would have clocked it and made sure she was safe. Instead, you stood there yelling over your bruised pride." She tapped her heel against the floor, making a clicking sound. "Maybe you've been an Outlaw too long because you can't see your salvation when it's staring you in the face."

"How did that work out for you?" I asked, knowing she'd button up quickly. Her lips pursed, and I was in the clear. Angelica would stop pushing me. She never liked to be reminded how many times I'd pulled her ass out of the fire. "She dumped beer down my back." I huffed, drying my neck with the towel.

"Lulu said the father behind you had his hand on Roxy. That's why she froze, but you would rather assume the worst because it fits your narrative a little easier." She walked towards the door, placing her hand on the handle before she turned back towards me. "It was an accident. Get over it, because I can guarantee Roxy is trying to figure out where she went wrong."

***

I watched Roxy cross the street to the cheap motel, still dressed in her saloon uniform. There were a few catcalls, but she ignored them. I did not, threatening violence with a look at the offenders as I passed them. There were a few who wanted to test me, but one look at the patch on my back, and they thought better of it.

Who is she? One minute I thought I had her pegged as a rich daddy's girl, but nothing else fit that mold. Her car was a shitbox, and she waitressed like she was a veteran. A daddy's girl would never have set foot in this dump. I was no closer to the truth, and each piece I learned contradicted the one before. She was a puzzle, and I had all the wrong fucking pieces.

Roxy stopped in front of the third door on the second floor, and I crouched between two cars parked in the lot. She opened her purse and started digging for the skeleton key they actually gave the patrons here, but it was shit like this that made me think I was wrong. Any poor chick would have had the key in her palm, with the blade sticking out to cut a bitch.

Her door slammed shut, and I started the countdown.

Three minutes. Pulling my wallet out of my back pocket, I reached for the fake credit card I had stored for this exact purpose.

Two minutes. A smirk danced at the corner of my lips as I took the stairs one at a time to the second floor. I wanted to savor the anticipation.

One minute. It didn't take long to reach her door. Placing my ear against the grain, I listened for any sound. She should have been moving around the room, but there was nothing. Too quiet.

"What the fuck are you doing?" a man said from behind me. I hadn't been paying close enough attention, my heart pounding in my ears the closer I was to her door.

"I fucked up, and my Old Lady won't let me in." The words tasted like sawdust. Women were too much trouble, and I never saw myself actually committing to one. He didn't need to know the truth, and I didn't give a fuck if he bought it. He looked me up and down, decided it wasn't worth the fight, and continued past me until he reached the stairs.

Leaning against the door frame, I stayed in place until I couldn't see his back anymore. I could have taken him if he had been a threat, but if he ever met Roxy, he'd instantly believe I was in the doghouse. Shaking my head, I pushed my shoulder against the door, creating a gap.

The trick was simple—wedge the credit card in between the door and the jamb along the curved edge of the bolt, pushing it back into the door to unlock. I'd done this a thousand times, but when I heard the lock pop, I couldn't shove the door open. *What the fuck*?

The lock hadn't clicked back into place, but when I tried again to press the door open, it wouldn't move. These doors didn't have chains on them, and that was when it hit me. She'd stuck the desk chair underneath the handle, like that would protect her.

Kicking the door repeatedly, I created enough forward pressure to force the chair to slide to the floor. The door opened completely, and Roxy was leaning against the wall near the bathroom, wearing only a towel. She'd heard the door, and when she'd actually seen it was me, she went silent. It made me angry to think someone had taught her to be invisible.

I let go, letting the door slam. The walls were thin, and the sound echoed around the room. I wasn't a betting man, but even I'd play the odds nothing was sacred in this motel. My eyes never left her as I hauled the chair upright and dropped into it, planting myself between her and freedom. She wasn't going anywhere, and while I searched for fear in her eyes, there was only bone-deep exhaustion. I wasn't sure which was worse.

"If you want to go through my things, I don't care. Just don't touch my underwear. That's gross." She stood straight, heading toward a small suitcase lying on the floor before crouching down.

"Why don't you just tell me your story? The longer you keep this to yourself, the more suspicious it becomes." I'd sift through her things, but if she only had that little suitcase, there wouldn't be much to find.

"You don't see me asking for your story every two seconds." She stood before turning towards the bed to drop some clothes. Roxy grabbed the shirt, flinging it over her head until it came down past her waist. She quickly dressed, pulling the towel away from her before heading back to the bathroom. "I don't expect Aces to fix my car for free. Nothing is, but you couldn't even leave a buck after all the bullshit. Figures, I got stiffed."

"I actually gave Aces the money for your car." I didn't know why I was telling her this, when I didn't honestly care what she thought. The brothers had wanted to punish her for the beer, but when Angelica told me what had happened, I collected the money. It had been too late to give it to her, so I'd made a deposit towards her car.

"If you each left a dollar or two, that's not enough to pay for the repairs. You should have given it to me. I'm an adult, and I know how to balance my finances. Shocking!" She leaned against the wall again, staring straight at me.

"Why are you angry? You're going to have to pay for your repairs, and all I did was make a deposit."

"It wasn't your decision. If you wanted to stiff me, fine. I can't control what people think of my services. I'm an adult, and I can take care of myself." She glared at me, crossing her arms over her chest.

I didn't flinch, returning her gaze. "So, are you going to tell me your story?"

"There's nothing interesting to tell. I'll be gone in a few weeks, and you won't even remember I was here." She yawned, not covering the exasperation with me.

"Scorpion's worried you're bringing something into town that's going to affect Angelica. She takes in strays, and it's happened before. That's why I'm here, so that he doesn't take it upon himself to get answers his way." I shifted in the chair, studying her.

She'd been dolled up for the saloon, but now her hair hung loose, black and messy, falling to her shoulders. Her eyes were exhausted, like she'd seen some shit, and tonight, she couldn't hide her pain.

"Look," she said, walking towards me until she reached the edge of the bed, turning down the bedspread that had seen better days. "I'm leaving as soon as Aces fixes my car. Goodnight." When she placed one knee onto the bed, that was when I saw it.

The sleep shorts shifted, showing the red fingerprints on her upper leg.

My nostrils flared, and all I saw was red as I tried to force air into my lungs, not letting her see how much this was rattling me. She'd thought silence was the answer, but in our world, it was violence.

The motherfucker had touched her.

Chapter Seven

A Thigh For A Thigh

Cactus

I said nothing to Roxy about the fingerprints, nor did she say anything to me about why I was still sitting in her room. She laid down, pulled the bedspread up, and crashed hard. As long as she was working for Angelica, she'd be under Saint's Outlaws' protection, which was the only reason I was here.

Her suitcase caught my eye as I focused on the room, remembering I was here to figure her out. I could go through her stuff for my sick gain, but I had a feeling I wouldn't find anything. There were mostly clothes sticking out and a few toiletries, but nothing that would tell me who she was or if she was running from anything.

Digging through her things was going to be a bust, but I could head back to the saloon. I knew which table the family had been sitting at, and it wouldn't have been that hard to pull their receipt. However, the club didn't have tracing capabilities, and this wasn't worth trading a favor for. I was coming close to a dead end, and that wasn't fucking acceptable to me either.

Letting out a frustrated moan, I slid back in my chair. I was batting 0 for 2, and I didn't have a fucking clue how I was going to fix any of this. I let my gaze roam around the room, but when I saw the check presenter, I had a feeling I had just gotten lucky. The saloon had a stack of check presenters at the main register, so the girls could just place the receipt in one and drop it off at the table. However, Angelica made sure each girl kept her own to track daily earnings. Roxy's was sitting on the edge of the cheap nightstand.

Although the lamp remained on, she didn't move as I quietly sat on the edge of the bed. Roxy didn't even twitch, and that pissed me off. She should never have crashed with me in the room. Her lack of self-preservation was a problem. She'd run into danger, head first, and Angelica would step in to defend her. It would force Scorpion to rear his ugly head. Roxy would pay, even if it hadn't been her fault.

Opening the presenter, I flipped through the receipts. Roxy had written her tip amounts, and she'd done pretty well considering it was the slow season. There were only two receipts she hadn't written on—ours and, by the table number, the family behind us. Shitty, but it didn't surprise me. There were pen marks bleeding through the receipt paper, so I flipped it over, needing to know what it said. The fucking asshole had written on the back: 'If you want your tip, call." There was a phone number. He'd be lucky if he was still alive by the end of the night. This was a slight to the club, and that shit never stood.

Taking my phone out, I snapped a picture, smirking at the idea that was forming.

"Hey," I whispered to Roxy's back, not bothering to check to see if she was faking. I didn't fucking care either way. "You're racking up favors, and I always collect. Starting with the beer."

I left, waiting until I turned the corner, away from the motel, before I pulled out my phone.

"Yo," Huckleberry answered on the first ring.

"You getting any?" I asked, needing to know if he was actually going to be helpful. Otherwise, I'd have to head back to the clubhouse before executing my plan.

"Not yet, but there's a few extra girls here, if you want one."

I laughed. "Pick one for yourself, and she can thank me later. I need you to help me deal with a certain problem from this afternoon."

"Fucker touched her? I thought that was a joke." Huck was a lot. He could flip through his seven personalities quicker than I could lace up my boots, but there was one thing he didn't stand for. No one fucked with the women in his life, and while Roxy wasn't his, she was a part of the saloon. Close enough.

"Saw the handprint." I let that settle in, knowing it would rile him up.

"What do you want to do?"

"He left Roxy his phone number, so I'm hoping you can use the girl to set something up. People will miss him, but you know he's done this before." This would be the last time he'd touched without permission.

"Yeah, send me the number, and I'll take care of it."

The phone went dead in my hand, but I'd reached my bike, parked in the saloon's back lot. Sitting, I sent him the picture I'd taken and waited. Huck didn't disappoint me, calling me back in under ten minutes.

"I had my chick call the fucker, and he picked up on the first ring. Told her he couldn't really talk, so I had her give him the address for the motel in Bisbee. Room 100 hasn't seen action in a while."

"When we're done, fuck her real good. She earned it." I laughed, knowing exactly where he'd sent the fucker. We had a permanent rental for the room with the owner under a false name for situations like this. "I'll meet you over there."

I was still laughing as I started my bike, pulling out onto the road.

***

This was the epitome of a shitty fucking motel room. Roxy's room was a palace compared to this dump. At least she had actual furniture, even if it was cheap. Everything in this room except the bed was cardboard, and I knew of at least one time when a brother had fallen through the dresser, destroying it.

It didn't fucking matter that the bed had sheets but no bedspread. I wasn't sure what fluids were seeping into the mattress, and I wasn't taking the risk. I'd like to see my fiftieth birthday. However, the room was perfect for what we used it for, and if we spilled blood tonight, all it would take was one phone call to the cleaning crew. I didn't mind blood. I just didn't bleach.

I was standing in the corner of the room when Huck signaled our visitor was here. There was a light rap on the door. I took one more step back into the shadows, and Huck used the door to hide behind as he opened it. The fucker walked in like he was planning on getting his and getting the fuck out.

"It's getting late, and I didn't think you would call..."

I didn't give a fuck how late it was at all. If he cared about his family, he would never have touched Roxy.

Huck let the door slide shut, knocking the man to the ground. "She didn't call you, fucker."

"What the fuck?" The man rolled onto his back, looking up at Huck. He wasn't innocent, and like I told Huck, I had a gut feeling this wasn't the first time the man on the ground had done this. It was just the first time he'd ever gotten caught. "Man, I don't want any trouble. I thought you were the waitress."

"That's where you fucked up." I stepped forward, making my presence known.

"Look," he said, holding his hands up to placate us. "My wife's a bitch. She's making me take this historical vacation for the kids, when all I wanted to do was go to Vegas."

"So, you thought you could touch without permission? It'd get her all hot, and she'd let you wet your dick? For what? Twenty bucks?" I let my temper flare, still deciding if this man was going to die tonight. If we killed him, no one would find him buried underneath a cactus in the desert. Hell, his wife would probably thank us if she knew.

"It was a lapse in judgement. I promise never to do it again." The man tried to stand, but Huck put a boot to his chest.

"You'll never do it again." Huck raised his boot, kicking him between the legs. It was so swift, the man sprang up, trying to curl into a ball to relieve the pain. Huck planted one of his boots on the man's chest again, pinning him to the ground. "How far do you want to go?" he asked me.

"Let's see, I saw four red marks. You get one more, and I get two." I thought it sounded fair.

"You should teach your boys how to be men." Huck removed his foot, rolling the man over onto the nasty carpet. He grabbed the man's wallet from his back pocket. "Repeat after me..." he said, pocketing his driver's license. "...David." Huck pulled back his foot, kicking the man in the balls from the back this time. "Consent is sexy, bitch."

I couldn't help the laughter that bubbled from my chest. "I've been on the opposite end of his kicks," I said, grabbing the man's hair and forcing him to look at me while I pointed at Huck. "You'll be lucky if you piss straight after a week."

Contemplating where I wanted to leave my mark, I thought about the fingerprints on the back of Roxy's leg.

In theory, this should work, but I had never tried to jump on the back of someone's upper thigh before. A thigh for a thigh seemed the decent way to go. Placing my boot in the same location he'd left a mark, I jumped, landing with all of my weight against. *Crunch*. The man wore shorts, and when I went to look at my handiwork, it was pretty gnarly. "Something's definitely broken," I sang.

"He's not screaming." Huck jiggled the bottom of the man's foot with his. "I think you might have knocked him out. That had to hurt."

"Pussy. I'm wondering if we should do his wife a favor." I didn't care either way.

"No," he moaned, his head rolling so that his cheek lay on the carpet. "I'll be a good boy. Please."

"Do you believe this shit?" I asked Huck.

"Not really, but my hard-on is going soft, and I've got a blonde waiting for me."

"Don't say I've never done you any favors, you sick fuck." I put my boot back on top of the mess I had created, jumping again. The man's screams reverberated around the room, and Huck sniffed the air, as if they were the best aphrodisiac.

I grabbed the man under one arm, and Huck grabbed the other. We dumped him in his car, but before I closed the door, I issued one last warning. "You hired a girl, and her man robbed you for touching without permission. You learned your lesson and won't try that again. Drive yourself home. If you're found here, the story will be even more believable." I held my hand out for his wallet. He had five hundred in cash, and I'd give it to Aces to go towards Roxy's car. She needed to hit the road, getting the fuck out of Tombstone and never looking back.

My work here was done.

Chapter Eight

Doc Holliday Saves The Day

Roxy

I plastered a bright smile on my face as the front door to the saloon opened from the outside. The breakfast crowd, if you could call it that, had left a few hours ago, and we hadn't had a customer since. I was ready to ham it up for a tip, but my smile slid when Angelica and her daughter walked in.

"Mom," her daughter moaned, "why can't Dad pick me up?"

"Your dad is leaving town, and after that stunt last night, you're never staying home alone again," Angelica sighed, her eyes sweeping the empty dining room before landing on Lulu and me. We were leaning against the back counter. "Did Francene leave?"

"Yeah, she said to call her if we got busy, and she'd come back, but..." Lulu raised her hands, spreading them out towards the dining room.

Angelica gracefully weaved between the tables, with the girl following in her footsteps. The closer they came, the easier it was to see the familial resemblance. She had her mother's face, but it was her eyes that drew me in, dark, almost black. "Bri, this is Roxy," Angelica introduced us, and I gave the girl a quick wave. "Roxy, this is my daughter, Bri. She's fourteen going on thirty, so please encourage her to stay in school and leave the boys alone." She rolled her eyes, making sure Bri wasn't watching.

I smiled, remembering when I'd been her age. I'd mostly raised myself, and it hadn't been easy, but I'd survived.

"Nice to meet you," she grumbled, waving back at me. "My mom said I had to help, but you don't have any customers, so this sucks ass."

"Your father may let you use that language, but I don't. Knock it off." Angelica shook her head, mouthing, *Help me!*

I held my chuckle in, but Lulu wasn't as lucky. "What did you do to deserve such torment?"

"Do you want to tell them, or would you like me to?" Angelica shot Bri a look. Whatever the girl had done was bad enough to get the universal mom death stare. Even my mother had perfected one when she was sober enough to remember she had a daughter.

"I tried to go to a party." Bri crinkled her nose while crossing her arms.

"Where was the party?" Angelica prompted, nudging Bri with her elbow.

I kept quiet, but it wasn't hard to figure out that this party had involved a boy. It wasn't my place to say anything, but if I got the chance, I'd play big sister later if Bri wanted to talk. She didn't know me, and sometimes that made it easier to confide. Bad boys weren't worth it, and good ones never peer pressured you into what they wanted.

"Honey, where was it?" Lulu prompted when Bri buttoned up her lips.

"She was supposed to be staying with a friend, but Cactus and Huckleberry found her in Boot Hill Cemetery. They broke up the party and called me. Thank God the kids weren't drinking, but there was alcohol." Angelica shook her head, her eyes wide as she told this part of the story.

Lulu talked with her hands. "Honey, next time you're going to sneak out, head to—"

"Lulu!" Angelica quickly shut her up, but I couldn't help the laughter that exploded from my chest. "Bri can't stay home alone, so you get an extra helper."

"Is it always this slow?" I winked at Bri as I changed the subject.

"It's summer," she answered me, like it was obvious, and I should have known that. She walked towards the kitchen door, pushing it open. "I'm getting a snack. This totally blows."

"You're so lucky your dad wasn't the one to find you, Bri. Scorpion wouldn't have just broken up the party." Angelica huffed at the swinging door, as if Bri could still hear her.

"No wonder her eyes looked familiar." I had seen that shade before, except those eyes had been cold and unyielding.

"Yeah, he didn't always have a stinger." Her head swiveled towards the kitchen door, making sure it was still closed. "This summer hasn't been too bad, but I never expected to walk into this."

"What time is it?" Lulu asked, standing on her tiptoes, trying to see the old-fashioned clock above the bar. "The city pays re-enactors to relive the fight at the O.K. Corral. They start the skirmish at the far end of the street, and if we get out there in time, we can join the show." Lulu clapped, spinning on her toes. "Come on, Roxy. Time to bag a cowboy. Do you want a Clanton or an Earp?"

"Is one better than the other?" I was confused, but I would follow her lead. I hoped I wouldn't make too much of a fool of myself, but it wasn't like we were making money today.

"I prefer the outlaws with the red sashes." She winked, laughing as she pulled me towards the front door.

"Don't get me fined," Angelica called after us. "I'm serious."

The door closed behind us, and Lulu perched against one of the support beams for the boardwalk. I went to stand next to her, but she shooed me towards the other one. "If you don't want to say anything, it's okay. I can do this."

People on the street stopped, and a pit in my stomach formed. I didn't like not knowing what would happen, and according to Lulu, we were about to be the center of attention.

Two men stumbled down the street, pretending to be drunk as they raised empty bottles in the air. "I'm not drunk. Ole Wyatt can't see straight. Maybe he's drunk," the younger of the two said. He took a step forward, pretending to trip over his feet, but righting himself at the last minute.

"He's not taking my gun away from me. I don't care what he says. No one appointed him God," the older man chimed in, taking a fake swig from the bottle.

"Now boys, you know the Earps don't mess around." Lulu leaned against the pole, her hand behind her head, sticking her leg out in a pinup pose.

"You're trouble, Lulu. I've got enough trouble floating around this town."

She shifted, twirling a piece of her hair between her fingers and batting her eyelashes. "I don't know what you're talking about, Ike. You know, you could come have a drink with me at the Blue Angel."

I had to hand it to Lulu. Every eye on the street was on her and not the men still stumbling around. I wish I was exaggerating, but I could feel their eyes on me as I leaned against the pole across from her.

"Nope, I've got stuff to do. I know your little game." He stopped, right in front of her.

"Maybe next time." She giggled.

The men continued down the street, hamming it up, but I noticed no one else joined in. If these people actually came to the saloon, I wouldn't lose any money for the day. I had car repairs to think about, but I didn't want to ask Aces how much. I figured if I saved whatever I could, it would be alright, and I'd leave before the end of the month. No matter what, I wasn't staying. This place made small towns feel like metropolises.

"Those were the Clantons," Lulu quickly described. "The next round of men will be the three Earps and Doc Holliday. They're kind of interchangeable, but Doc has a cane." She twirled a strand of hair around her finger. "The show tells the story of how the law settled Tombstone. Are you all right?"

I nodded at her, taking in the crowds of people on the boardwalk. It wasn't long before we heard more men coming down the street. I swore there was sweat dripping down my back underneath the corset, but these men wore black frock coats with black cowboy hats. They had to be dying.

"Did anyone see anything suspicious?" one man called out. "We got a report that some cowboys are drunk with guns." He must have been one of the Earps, per Lulu.

Lulu kept quiet, so I did too. I knew little about the place, but I was glad she'd given me a crash course between the rounds of men. I didn't feel so lost watching the show.

The Earps all looked the same with their puffed-out chests, but I recognized the actor playing Doc Holliday. He shuffled down the street with his cane, just as Lulu had said. His eyes shifted back and forth until they met mine.

"You're new in town," he drawled, pointing his cane at me as he neared. "See anything you should be reportin', darlin'?" *Why me? I couldn't fuck this up. We needed customers.*

"No, sir. I would tell you if I had. Lulu and I came out to get some air." I matched his energy, internally shitting bricks. I was going to kill Lulu, but I must have been doing something right because I caught her wink out of the corner of my eye.

"You sure, girl?" He smirked at me.

"Roxy, sir." I went for a wide-eyed, innocent look. *More like the scared saloon girl.* "I don't want any trouble, Mr. Holliday."

"I hear there's some vermin hanging around town. You should get back to the Blue Angel." He tipped his cowboy hat at me before walking away. He was only a few steps down the street when he called over his shoulder. "Better keep my seat warm at the bar, Roxy."

We waited until the crowd moved with them before heading back inside.

"Damn, girl, you don't know what you've just done." Lulu held my hands, jumping up and down, but she let me go when I wasn't jumping with her.

"What happened?" Angelica emerged from the kitchen.

"Doc Holliday told Roxy to keep his seat warm at the bar."

They both squealed, and I had to stick my fingers in my ears.

Angelica instantly made plans. "I'm not calling Francene back. You two can split the room, and the tips should make up for the slow morning. I'll bus and run food, and Bri can be the hostess. No one will say anything about the wait if she's at the front door." She clapped her hands, doing a spin move as her brown hair twirled out from behind her.

"What are you two on?" I was utterly confused.

"Doc Holliday is having lunch here." Lulu grinned, eyes full of excitement. "Every tourist is going to fight for a table just to see him."

A full restaurant meant tips. If the car was ready next week, I could leave sooner than I planned. This place was a time warp, and I wasn't letting it trap me.

Chapter Nine

Trapped in Tombstone

Cactus

My burner phone rang, but I ignored the vibrations coming from my ass, not giving a fuck which brother it was. I couldn't get it through their thick skulls that they needed to knock it the fuck off. Each time one of them called for something stupid, they were giving away the club run's position.

"Are you going to answer that?" Tumbleweed moved the chew into his other cheek before he smiled at me. His teeth were streaked brown from the shit, and there were always glasses lying around the clubhouse with his spit in them. I tried to tell him he'd get caught at some crime scene over the fucking stuff, but he just laughed at me.

I wanted to push his bike over and let it pin him to the dirt. He would see it coming, and it would be more trouble than it was worth. After the last drop-off, we'd camped in an RV park overnight, making sure we were early for today's pickup.

I shook my head, not bothering to answer. It didn't matter where we were going or what business we had. If Scorpion scheduled a run, I was on it, and that fucker liked to stack as many as he could into a short amount of time.

I rolled my eyes, internally moaning and groaning some more. Scorpion hated me because I'd forced him to step up and be a man until he had outranked me. I didn't care for him because he always chose excuses over his family. Now he held more power, and the line between us was razor thin.

We were at the pickup location, our bikes sitting in formation on a narrow dirt road, engines cut. Out in the desert, silence wasn't peace—it was a warning. We could hear anyone coming for miles. Most of us wore open-faced skullcaps for helmets, so we didn't need to remove them.

It wasn't hard to figure out why the brothers bothered me. We lived surrounded by violence, and no one from this chapter had ever made it to their forty-first birthday. I had ten months to go, and every brother knew it. Some of them wanted to make sure I was alive, others, to keep track of my location in case they had to claim my body. Add in my beef with Scorpion, and it was a clusterfuck waiting to blow. Knowing my luck, today was the day.

The wind kicked up enough that it danced along the brush on the side of the road, spinning up dust devils.

I'd been a nomad, stuck somewhere west of the Mississippi River, the first time Angelica had called in a panic. I hadn't expected her to break down, and it had haunted me ever since.

"Grant," she had cried, "I need your help. Dad's going to kill Brice if he finds out I'm pregnant."

The silence pressed harder, and my mind replayed the conversation word-for-word as if it was happening all over again in my ear.

"I told you to stay away from him," I could hear myself say. Brice had been the kid down the street with his own military father to deal with, but where ours had been overly ambitious, his had been a violent drunk.

"You don't know him like I do," she'd grumbled, and I could imagine the stubbornness settling on her face.

"I know he's never going to man up to support you. How is he going to be a father when he can't even wipe his own ass?" I wouldn't allow anyone to tear down Angelica. My mother had suffered enough through my father's ambitions. I couldn't sit and watch as my sister suffered a similar fate. "I'll come home," I had said, the memory fading as I heard Tumbleweed trying to speak to me.

"What if it's your girl?" Tumbleweed asked. He'd finally decided that he was well enough to get out of bed and do his fucking job. As road captain, like me, he didn't have a choice. He was the best tracker I'd ever known, and he knew these trails better than the coyotes.

"She doesn't have my number," I said, not even having to think which girl he meant. Tumbleweed and the rest of the brothers started laughing hysterically, and that was when I figured out I had fucked up. There were loose lips in the clubhouse, which was why most of the brothers knew about Roxy, but only the ones at lunch had known about the car.

"When are you going to bring her around?" He shifted in his seat, getting comfortable. He'd be sorely disappointed if he thought I was going to gossip with him.

"Why would I?" I snapped. I knew no one else would say anything. Tumbleweed had his fun, and the rest of the brothers got to listen in for a few seconds. I wasn't angry at them, knowing they only saw Roxy as a woman to conquer.

My phone started vibrating again, and the brothers thought it was the funniest thing ever. "What?" I roared, answering it.

"Seriously? I'm doing you a favor. The least you could do is say thank you. Bitch," Aces spat back at me.

"What the fuck do you want? This better not be a social call."

"Yeah, well, your girl has been calling the shop since you've been gone. Probably wants to know about her car, but hasn't shown up to actually ask." Aces snorted. "At least she's not leaving messages, like the single mommies do."

I shook my head, trying not to strangle him through the phone. Aces had a reputation for playing rough. The women in town thought he was a dom. They were always sadly mistaken when they realized he was just another asshole with a fetish, but it never stopped them from trying.

"What's wrong with it, fuckwit?" I wasn't a patient man, which made me good at tracking down enemies of the club, but I was out of fucks to give today, and Aces was towing a very thin line.

"Cracked radiator."

"How bad?" I really wanted to know how much it was going to cost to fix and how long it would take him, but he was drawing this out for his entertainment.

"Not bad. She has a couple of cracks that I can fix. As long as there's nothing serious we didn't see, I should be able to get her out of here by the middle of next week. The five hundred you gave me from the douche will cover most of it, but she'll still need a couple hundred more."

I might have given him the go-ahead, but I wanted more time, telling myself it was because I didn't have her story yet. "Nah. Tell her she blew the head gasket, and you're going to have to order parts. You don't know when they'll come in."

"Fuck," Aces snorted. "Are you planning on keeping your new toy? Because if you're not..."

"She's a saloon girl, and we don't shit where we eat." It was the truth. As long as she worked in the saloon, she was off-limits. It was the easiest way to protect her from unwanted attention.

"Rude." The line clicked as he hung up in my ear.

Tumbleweed leaned back on his bike. "For a man who doesn't want a commitment, you sure are putting obstacles in her path to stay."

I laid my arms across my handlebars, soaking in the stillness. It stretched on too long, but before I could say anything to Tumbleweed, he shot up from lying across the back of his bike. I followed his line of sight, but I couldn't see what had caused the shift. I didn't discredit him, though. Something had caught his attention because Tumbleweed never cried wolf.

"The ground is rumbling, and I don't like it," he said, pulling out the binoculars he stored in his saddlebags. I waited, along with the other brothers, knowing he had this under control, our keys ready to turn on our bikes at a moment's notice. "The cargo trucks that we're supposed to be escorting are back-to-back, overloaded. That's probably why the ground is rumbling. The cartel loves us, so they don't pay based on weight. Strictly reputation and delivery."

"Quit dragging your boots, and spit it out."

He hadn't relaxed in his seat. "There are four crotch rockets following them."

"What the fuck? Hijack?" I asked. "Those trucks are running cargo. They're just trying to escape the taxes at the border. If they wanted the guns or drugs, they should have pulled this off at the beginning of the week." I pulled my bandana over my mouth, preparing to raise some hell.

"I don't know, but I plan on getting some answers. There's more of us than them." Tumbleweed adjusted his bandana. "If we ride straight for the trucks, they won't see us."

"Alright, we're going to have to surround them."

I didn't believe in ghosts, the afterlife, or any of that fucking bullshit, but it looked like I might meet the Grim Reaper after all.

Fuck me.

Chapter Ten

Too Old For This Shit

Cactus

Today wasn't a fucking good day to die—unless I got to take a few motherfuckers with me. Tomorrow wasn't fucking promising either.

The thought rattled around in my skull as I rode straight for the first truck. Tumbleweed's front tire chewed up dust, the grit settling over my helmet, mixing with the sweat dripping down my forehead. It would be my fucking luck if it slid down my sunglasses, blinding me. *Why the fuck couldn't this have happened in the winter?*

The Saint's Outlaws had always played by our own rules, but we hadn't updated with the times. Our reputation preceded us, but I was wondering if there was a better way. We still traded favors for information, banking on actually being sold the truth. There were no fancy gadgets or computers. Just sheer aggression.

If I don't fucking get crunched between Tumbleweed and the truck, she's buying me dinner. Steak.

This was it, and I made sure my right hand gripped the middle of my handlebars to control the bike. Crooking my left elbow, I held it out, hoping Tumbleweed was fucking paying attention. I didn't feel like flying headfirst over my bike, landing in some prickly green shit along the side of the narrow road. I wouldn't be able to dig myself out, and then the brothers would never let me live it down.

This was supposed to be the easiest part of the week—no drugs, no guns, just cargo. Grab the money, get paid and celebrate with a few fucks. Yet, we were preparing for battle, and I desperately wanted to pound my fists into something or someone. I didn't care which at the moment, as long as I could feel the sting as my knuckles broke open. It wouldn't release the anger increasingly rising within me, but it sure sounded like fun. My fingers curled in against my palm, my fist forming.

The trucks hadn't decreased their speed, and I could see the driver of the first one yelling from the inside. *I don't get paid enough for this fucking shit.* It wasn't hard to guess he was swearing up a storm, his hands directly pointing in our direction. If I weren't in the middle of saving his ass, I'd pull my piece and pop his tires, and then maybe he would learn a little respect. The first driver in the caravan was always the most experienced one. If he was panicking, I could only imagine how the second driver was fucking coming apart at the seams.

I was a bike length from the front when I stuck my fist directly out, sliding towards the left. Tumbleweed did the same, taking the right. He was actually paying the fuck attention.

I rode as close as I could to the side of the truck, not wanting to be dragged underneath. It wasn't ideal, but I also didn't need the bikes following the trucks to have a clear view of me either. I didn't analyze how we were going to get out of this scenario. We always worked better on the fly, making shit up as we went.

I passed the back of the first truck, but when I looked up into the cab, the second driver had both hands threaded in his hair, pulling at the roots to make it stand up on end. I couldn't decide whether he was angry or scared. His lips moved, but it might have been in prayer. The two of them had clearly lost the plot, forgetting who their saviors were.

I'm too old for this fucking shit.

Sliding towards the edge of the narrow road, I scanned the surrounding area, looking for the bikers. Tumbleweed had said they were there, but I didn't see a fucking thing. No clouds of dust heading my way. No obnoxious engine sounds besides ours and the truck's. *What the fuck is going on?*

If Tumbleweed got this wrong, he was going to be the one to feel my fists. I'd be gentle, focusing only on sprains, not breaks. As long as he could still get it up, the club bunnies would take pity.

Think Roxy will play naughty nurse?

A shot rang out, hitting the brush next to me. Another shot ricocheted off the top of the truck, bouncing off the right side, but I didn't hear any screams, so it must not have hit. I was a little disappointed Tumbleweed had gotten this right. I'd been looking forward to pounding his flesh.

Someone had been following the trucks, and instead of calling for backup, the drivers had pretended they didn't exist. There'd be hell to fucking pay when we got out of this. They had to have known they were being followed.

A bullet hit the cactus I had just passed, and I slid closer to the side of the truck. I wasn't afraid to die, just didn't want to call it too fucking early. I couldn't be worried about the brothers behind me. They should have been paying attention, and if they ran each other over, we'd replace them. Problem fucking solved.

It wasn't until I reached the back of the second truck that I saw the crotch rockets. There were four of them, two in the front and two in the back. Pulling my piece from the back of my jeans, I waited.

Shots rang out, but I didn't bother firing back. I was too far away, and the chances of actually hitting something from this angle were slim to none. If I fired and missed, it would just give them a better target to nail my ass.

Clearing the back of the truck, I aligned my bike with the back left corner of the overhead door. It was creating a nasty crosswind, but I was an experienced rider. It wasn't anything I couldn't handle, more annoying than anything else. As I moved in the opposite direction, it died down, and I could focus on the bikes directly in front of me. Tumbleweed caught my eye as he maneuvered next to me on the right. The rest of the brothers would line up behind us once they passed the truck.

Tumbleweed made sure I was watching as he raised his hand. He had two fingers stuck together, and then he split them apart. It wasn't a bad plan. He wanted us to ride straight towards them, and when we were close enough, split.

Easy if it worked, bloody if we missed our opportunity. If we could surround them, we might have a chance of heading home unscathed. We had the numbers, and they wouldn't be so fucking lucky if we pulled this off.

We rode forward, clocking the distance until the split. My mind was racing. *Why hadn't they sped up?* They were still riding at the same, even pace as when we'd first seen them. *They're still in formation?* It would have been easier for them to play chicken with us. Yet they stayed, making it easier for us to see our next move.

Tumbleweed nodded at me, seeing the same strategy I had. There were two crotch rockets in each line, but they'd left the middle wide open. There was plenty of room for him and me to split them, cutting off any communication they had. As long as the other brothers took the outside, this was a better plan.

Multiple shots rang out, but once I stopped clutching my ass cheeks, it was easier to see they had orders to carry out. They weren't looking to clear us, and it made me even more suspicious. Their shots continued to ring out, one right after another, but they never aimed directly at us. In fact, they were shredding cacti along the roadside—prickly plant pieces flying everywhere. They needed a new strategy if they thought this was going to shake us.

Two bike lengths.

I held my left arm out, letting the brothers behind me know to take the outside. *Don't fuck this up.*

One bike length to go.

I hauled ass to get in front of Tumbleweed. I could feel him, his bike pounding the lane behind me. The exhilaration threaded up and down my spine, but everything else seemed to slow down. The lane didn't close, and I rode in between the first two crotch rockets.

Kicking the front tire of the biker to my left, I waited to see what would happen. A kick wouldn't have done anything to an experienced rider. They might have wobbled a little, but nothing serious. The biker I kicked laid his bike down in the dirt. It was so sudden, his buddy behind him couldn't avoid the mess and ran over his legs. The bike trapped his upper body.

There was no fucking chance in hell I was going to nail the second biker. I passed him, looking for somewhere to turn around. As I scanned my right side, thinking I could pull around the last biker in a wide swoop, Tumbleweed kicked his front tire. It wasn't really a kick. He used his foot as a lever, continually putting pressure on the tire until the rider couldn't maintain control. He rode off into the brush, and one brother on the right went after him.

I cleared the mess, but when I turned around, I couldn't help but laugh. Whatever this fucking was, it was obvious we'd won. Two of my brothers pinned the rider who had run over his buddy's legs to the ground. His bike was on its side, and there was no way he was going to move it without breaking a body part. On the right side, a brother held a gun to the last biker's head. No one flinched. We were used to this, but I couldn't help but wonder how much longer until my time fucking ran out.

Throwing my leg over my bike, I was preparing to interrogate our prisoners when the truck drivers stormed up the road, guns pointing. They had stopped their trucks further up, and now they thought they were going to be two badasses. I didn't even bother to raise my gun. If they'd been thinking straight, they should have taken off, letting us catch up to them.

"You imbeciles," the first one screamed, waving his gun in the air. These weren't cartel pros, just frightened men who were clinging onto a paycheck they would never see if they didn't deliver. "They're supposed to protect us." An icy chill slid down my spine. It didn't come from fear, no, it came from how goddamn dumb they were.

I motioned for a few of the brothers to work their way behind the truck drivers. They were so focused on me, they didn't see we were caging them in.

"What the fuck are you talking about?" I asked. There was no hint in my tone that something was amiss.

"They were supposed to protect us. Now, who's going to make sure we're safe?" He flung his hands around, the gun flailing. "I don't get paid enough for you to rob us."

"If you thought we were going to rob you, you should have kept driving, and we would have caught up. Put the fucking gun down." I didn't need to take a stray bullet. He didn't move quickly enough. The brothers standing behind him disarmed both of them, forcing them into the dirt. I wasn't worried about fucking around with the cartel. They cared more about the cargo than the drivers. If something happened to these two, there would be two more to replace them.

"Sit on him, and hold his head up," I commanded, but when I saw the driver's squinty eyes, I kicked a little dirt in his face. He coughed, cornered. "What the fuck is going on?"

They remained silent.

"Look, unless you can come up with some reasonable explanation, we're going to take your cargo and leave your body out here to rot." I wasn't just threatening them. That was exactly what was going to happen. I kicked a little more dirt when he didn't start talking right away.

"We followed the instructions. Picked up the cargo and drove it through the border. No one stopped us on the way here, but they showed up about ten miles back. They said to meet bikers. Figured they were you." After all the years riding with the Saints, I was an excellent judge of character. The trucker was telling the truth, even though he hadn't thought this through in the moment.

"You're not new to this. They never let the new guy in the first truck, so you had to have known we wear club cuts. We don't have full-shield helmets, and most of us would rather die than ride a crotch rocket. Pay attention the next time you pick up stragglers." I kicked more dirt just to be an asshole.

"Cactus," Tumbleweed called, waving his hand to get my attention. "Come here."

I headed in his direction. He was standing over the rider buried underneath his bike, probably paralyzed.

"They're all dead. Must have taken some sort of pill. There's foam in his mouth, so I'm not bothering with the rest, but we searched for IDs." Tumbleweed kicked the man's wrist. "The only identifying marks they have are these tattoos. It's a phoenix, but no one recognizes the significance. I took a picture.

It's in the same spot, on the inner wrist, for all of them. Club? Gang? Who the fuck knows."

I shook my head, knowing we wouldn't piece this together. "The driver said they crossed the border, and these four pulled in from behind. They thought they were us," I explained.

"Do you buy that shit?" Tumbleweed rubbed at his bottom lip, like he was some sleuth, cracking the case.

"Yeah, at least some of it. The drivers are just doing what they were told. They didn't have a clue, which was why they were yelling at us when we rode towards them. Who the fuck knows what's going on."

"Should we still deliver? I don't want to walk into a trap."

"I don't want to either, but I'm going to step away and call Scorpion. He needs to know what happened, and we'll go from there."

"Good luck." Tumbleweed walked away as I pulled out my phone.

Dread coiled in my gut as I dialed Scorpion's cell phone. My president needed to know what we were facing, but I wasn't confident in his ability to lead. If he chose wrong, it was our lives on the line, not his.

Chapter Eleven

Fucked And Not Kissed

Cactus

Heading towards the front of the first truck, I checked my signal. I had only two bars. *Good enough.* I dialed immediately, wanting to get this over with. Mesquite had still been president when I'd petitioned the Tombstone chapter for full-time patched-in status. He'd agreed, but knowing our history, he had made sure Scorpion and I were never on the same run. Mesquite had claimed someone had to stay back to protect Ang and Bri. Bullshit. He hadn't trusted us not to kill each other.

A loud female moan sounded as the phone clicked. Pulling it away from my ear, I checked to make sure I'd actually dialed Scorpion's number. No mistake.

It was this shit that fucking pissed me off. The brothers and I had risked our lives, taking care of club business, and our president was busy fucking some chick—a blonde because he never picked a brunette—whose name he'd forget as soon as she was warming another brother's bed.

"Seriously? I'm standing in the middle of the goddamn fucking desert doing your dirty work, and you're busy getting your dick wet." I was livid.

"You could have stayed a nomad."

"If you had taken care of your family, I would still be a nomad." I aimed low, not quite striking as hard as I had planned. I could hear flesh smacking against more flesh. Repeatedly. There were moans and groans every so often, and I didn't have to ask if I was on speaker. The sounds were too distinguishable for me not to be.

"Stay out of my business, or I might have to pay a visit to a certain new waitress. She's fair game." The words shot through me, forcing me to take a step back, but the truck grill didn't allow me to move. The woman screeched with pleasure in my ear as my teeth ground against each other. Scorpion had done it on purpose, knowing exactly how it would land. Roxy was in his sights, and she'd never see it coming until it was too late.

"Cargo's burned," I said, hanging up the phone as two loud moans reached my ears. Normally, listening in was hot, but I was so disgusted, it didn't even make me hard. Backing my butt against the truck's grill, I bent over, trying to gather my thoughts.

"He's busy, huh?" Tumbleweed leaned against the truck next to me. "He's doing that a lot. Focusing on his dick." He spat the snuff to the side before tucking the chew back into his cheek. "Did he say anything about this clusterfuck?"

I shook my head, not sure how much I wanted to reveal.

"He's spiraling, man. Everyone sees it. No one talks about it. Ang deserves happiness, and it ain't with him."

Tumbleweed's candor was throwing me off. No one said anything derogatory about Scorpion, either as a man or as our president. It just wasn't something that was done. I had had my suspicions for a while that there was dissent among the ranks. "Yeah, well, if she finds someone decent, I won't let him stand in her way." I slugged Tumbleweed in the arm. "Don't get any fucking bright ideas."

He laughed. "Nah, and I won't go for your girl either."

Roxy wasn't mine, but I didn't feel like fighting. "What do you want to do?" I asked him. "I'm inclined to leave the bikers here. They're dead already. Let the heat do the cleanup. We have a picture of their tattoos."

"Something's off. I played good cop. This is El Sombra Roja's shipment, and his men are normally better than this. The truckers don't even know what they're carrying. Someone had already loaded the cargo and told them to drive. That's why they didn't know the men behind them weren't us."

"I can't see this being a double-cross with the Red Shadow. Someone said he was taking care of business in California, and that's why he asked for full service with us. It could be delivery as normal if we show up at the warehouse." I scratched my beard. I'd rather take my chances meeting the Grim Reaper than show up at the clubhouse without the payment.

***

I was sitting on a stack of crates, dangling my legs back and forth as I watched the cartel inventory their cargo. Once we'd threatened the truck drivers to within an inch of their lives, the trip here had been uneventful. We'd surrounded them for protection. No one had been on the road, and when we rode up to the warehouse, it was business as usual. It made me wonder if the cartel knew about the bikers, or if this had just been a one-off we'd need to ask around about. There were too many directions, and I didn't like not having a concrete clue.

"Amigo," a heavy accent said from behind me. I was on high alert, swiveling my head to see who it was as I reached for my gun. I opened and closed my hand, searching for the piece, before I remembered I hadn't brought it. We'd left our pieces in our saddlebags out of respect for our clients.

"What are you doing on this side of the border?" I asked, settling down when the man stepped into the light. Javier Rodriguez, El Filo Negro, was a cartel nepo baby if I ever saw one. A gold chain that was at least two inches thick hung around his neck, dipping into the open collar of his five-hundred-dollar dress shirt. Cufflinks, not buttons, because a shirt that expensive cried out for the proper hardware. A suit that screamed cartel and shoes that were polished to the hilt.

"I'm ready to go home. I hate this heat, but duty calls, so here I am." He laughed, sitting on the cargo's corner nearest him.

"Seriously? It's the same heat." I raised an eyebrow, not sure who he thought he was fooling.

"It doesn't feel the same. The sweat drips down my back, and then there's a nasty wet stain between my ass cheeks." He shuddered.

I shook my head, not really believing I was discussing sweat with the Black Blade. He'd pull his gun out from behind him, only to kill his enemy with the slip of his wrist.

"Most of your brothers are with the girls, getting their fill before dinner. I had my chef grill steaks. Can't have our allies riding home with empty stomachs and full balls." He laughed again, crossing his arms over his barrel chest.

It was easier to change the subject, instead of offending him. I wasn't interested in emotionless sex, and there was nothing I could say that wouldn't reveal where my head was at. "I heard your uncle had business in California."

"He's strengthening connections." Javier leaned his elbow against his right thigh as his leg dangled. "Might as well spit it out, amigo."

I'd been a twenty-year-old kid, still riding with the Tombstone chapter, when I'd met Javier for the first time. He'd taken the omerta at fifteen, and while we weren't friends, I could stand to have a conversation with him every once in a while. A stillness settled between us as we watched his men unload the first truck.

"You know the Saints will never take over for the cartel. We're happy to take our piece of the pie." I didn't know how much I wanted to reveal, but I figured I might get some answers about today's fucked-up pickup.

"What happened?" Javier's leg still dangled as if he were content, but I only had to look at him to know he was really on high alert.

"We handled it, and I've already called Scorpion. He won't ask for more payment." I laid the groundwork, ensuring there was no animosity. The brothers would bitch if they didn't get to finish with the women the cartel kept upstairs for visitors. "There were four bikers riding behind your trucks when they met us at the checkpoint. We took care of them, but your drivers thought they were us, and there were some...misunderstandings."

"The drivers are still alive, so they couldn't have given you much fight."

"There was nothing we couldn't handle." It didn't matter what I said, he'd punish them and their handlers.

He made a noise as he rubbed his thumb against his bottom lip. "I'll put out some feelers and get back to you on what the actual story was. They should have known better." He'd beat the men involved within an inch of their lives until he got answers.

"Appreciate it." I pulled out my phone, bringing up the picture of the phoenix. "The bikers all had this on their wrists. Mean anything to you?"

"There's been rumors of a new biker gang. Yes, gang, before you say anything. They haven't been brave enough to fuck around and find out, but they hit a few of the lower-end street dealers. We don't protect them, since they're the bottom feeders. Send me the logo, and I'll see what I can find."

I nodded my head, not wanting to go further into detail, when we weren't necessarily in friendly territory.

"There's a woman upstairs for you, amigo. I made sure it's the one you always visit when you're here." He leaned over and bumped his elbow against mine.

"What am I going to owe you for bringing her?" I asked, playing along. This was the last delivery for the week, and I was tired. Too many runs, not enough quality sleep.

Javier laughed, slapping his hand over his knee. "Gift." He shook his head. "I brought her for me, but you look like you could use a good lay." I must have flinched because his smile widened. "Arranged marriage. I don't care what she does, and she turns a blind eye to my extramarital activities. It's the perfect marriage, but if I catch wind of the pool boy one more time, she's going to be missing a toy."

I couldn't help but chuckle. If Roxy even thought about entertaining one of those dumbass cowboys on the street, I'd put the fear of God into them. I had always been in the mood for easy pussy, but they took it to another level. They walked up and down the street for pay, providing an authentic Old West experience, but they really singled out the wives they thought they could nail. Roxy was better than that, and while I didn't think she'd ever believe their bullshit, I wasn't taking any chances.

"How long until dinner?" I asked. I was going to have to pay her a visit, but maybe if I timed this right, I wouldn't have to pretend I was interested.

"You've got about an hour, amigo." Javier smirked. "Should be enough time for your old ass."

"Look who's talking. This old ass saved yours." I let a smirk settle on my lips, standing up from where I'd been sitting on the cargo. "Send someone for me. You're cooking steaks. They're better than anything I could get in the clubhouse." I heard laughter follow me as I climbed the first couple of stairs, not sure how I was going to get out of the emotionless sex. I was fucking empty, and my dick knew it before I did.

Chapter Twelve

No Reason To Say Hello

Roxy

I checked on the family sitting at one of my tables before heading back to the kitchen to grab the next round of food.

The tourists wanted an Old West experience. The food was good, but that wasn't enough. They wanted the pictures, the atmosphere, and every nuance that came with the saloon. It never stopped, making most of the days feel the same—corset, shorts, and the same questions asking how to get a picture with the actors.

I had heard the other waitresses on the street were bitching about us. Most of the clientele chose the Blue Angel, leaving not much for anyone else. The customers they got weren't very nice. They wanted to grab a quick meal and go, often not leaving a tip.

"They can bitch all they want," Lulu had said the first time one of them had tried to start trouble. The low-cut saloon corset fit all our curves, but I swore Lulu had altered hers. She didn't spill over the top, but I often wondered how she kept it all locked down when she was one good bounce from disaster. Angelica shook her head, telling Lulu she'd pay the fine for indecency if there was one. I couldn't help but laugh, offering my usual service and saving the money in a plastic bag in my suitcase.

"Don't look now, but your buddy is about to walk through the door." Lulu sidled up to me, hooking her arm around mine for a second. "I don't know how you did it, but damn, girl. This is one of the best summers we've ever had."

"You told me to stay away from the cowboys." I chuckled at her antics, putting celery garnishes on the sandwiches I was getting ready to serve. "Don't get used to it. I won't be here next year, and you'll have to figure something else out." I quickly wondered where I would be at this time next year, but my vision went blank.

"Aces will never call you back, and you haven't gone to the garage to check on your car. I figure you're avoiding a certain biker, or you want to stay. Either way, I don't see you leaving Tombstone soon." She pulled away, bumping me with her hip before she went to greet the men. Doc was in his usual spot, Marshal Wyatt Earp beside him. The excitement was contagious as it buzzed throughout the room. The circus was back in town.

"I give it twenty minutes before every tourist is waiting for a table." Francene laughed. "Girl, I wish I had seen you."

"It wasn't a big deal," I whispered to her, grabbing the plates and heading for one table in the window. Francene wasn't exaggerating. The front door was opening every two seconds, and Bri was doing her best to get everyone on a waitlist. I had to give her credit. She was a sweet kid, but she didn't let anyone try to bully their way around her. We also watched out for her when any of us were near the front door.

"Lunch is served," I said, approaching the family sitting at the table. "Chicken tenders. Cook made them specially for you." I always said something directly to the kids. They were innocent, and I enjoyed watching them light up with joy while they still believed in something real.

"Ma'am?" the little boy asked. He still needed to use a booster chair to reach the table.

"Yes, cowboy?" I smiled back at him, laying the cheeseburger in front of his father, before moving around the table.

"Is that Mr. Holliday?" His little voice quivered as if he were in awe.

I served the rest of the food before I circled back around to him. Crouching to make sure we were on the same level, I gave him my full attention. "Yes, that is Mr. Holliday, and he's sitting next to Marshal Earp." I hadn't realized the saloon had gone quiet, listening in on my conversation with this little boy.

"Miss Roxy, would you do me a kindness?" Doc drawled, turning in his chair to face my general direction. I wasn't sure if he could see me, but it really didn't matter. This was about the little boy's curiosity.

"If you expect me to be nice to the Clantons, I will have to decline." I let my voice take the airy tone I'd used outside. There had already been two shows at the O.K. Corral, so I was pretty sure these people knew who I was talking about. "He forgets to pay his bill and snores at the bar." The room lit up with laughter.

"I would never subject a lady to such...poor standards." He smirked, clearly having fun playing to the crowd.

The men who played the Clantons stayed out on the street until it was time for their show, so I had no clue if that statement was even true. However, the room exploded, and I saw a few cell phones recording. It was family-friendly entertainment, and they were just making memories.

"I should probably be the one doing you a favor then." He smirked. "Would you be so kind as to bring that little cowboy over here? He needs to be deputized, as the marshal is getting old and senile." Doc knocked the actor playing Wyatt Earp in the arm with his cane.

"Do you want to meet Mr. Holliday and Marshal Earp?" I asked the little boy. If he was afraid, I'd figure something else out. I didn't want to see him traumatized on a family vacation. He said nothing, but he was old enough to unbuckle the strap of the booster chair, waiting for someone to lift him up.

"Do you have your phone with you so I can take a picture?" I whispered to his mother. She was stunned—half shocked, half trying not to cry. "If his food is cold, I'll take care of it when we get back." Reaching for the little boy, I set him down on the floor and held my hand out for him to hold. "Ready, cowboy?" He pulled me forward, knowing exactly how to get to the bar.

He stood between the men, waiting to see what was going to happen, but I took a few steps back to snap a few pictures for his mother. I'd been in Tombstone long enough to know they hadn't planned this, but it must have been a possibility because the marshal opened his suit coat, pulling out gold marshal stickers. They both stood from their bar stools, kneeling in front of the boy. The marshal said a few general words and stuck the sticker on his chest. They had officially deputized the kid. It was a cute moment, but it opened up the floodgates.

"What about my kid?" a mother snipped from near the side of the room. "We had to wait to be seated." She stood, pushing her kid towards the men, but she didn't see Lulu coming with a stack of plates. Lulu had to sidestep them, twirling to make sure the woman didn't knock all of them to the floor.

I hadn't meant for any of this to happen. I froze, standing there like a deer in headlights, until Angelica took over. She'd been standing in the hallway between her office and the dining room. "I'm sorry for your wait," she told the mother. "We do our best to be accommodating, but we never know when a visitor or two will drop in. I'm sure the men won't mind deputizing each kid who's currently in the room. There are way too many red sashes on the street."

The men each tipped their heads in her direction.

She spoke a few more words to the mother before calling me over. "Hey," she said, completely in control. I tried to apologize, but she waved me off. "It's alright, I'll grab an apron from my office and take over your tables. You're in charge of making sure each kid gets a few minutes with them. The food will be cold by the time they're done, but we can either remake it or send fresh with them." Angelica winked at me as she pivoted down the hallway.

For the next forty-five minutes, I led kid after kid up to be deputized. It was fun, but each time I saw Angelica with plates, my stomach crumbled. I should have been serving, not adding myself to the circus.

I tried to help Lulu for a second between kids, but she scolded me. "We're going to have a good day," she said, winking at me before rushing off.

I was walking the last kid back to their parents when the back of a motorcycle club cut caught my attention. Saint's Outlaws. Tombstone. My breath hitched as Cactus walked out the door. I hadn't even known he was here.

The door swung shut behind him, and I waited to see if he'd look through the windows. Nothing.

He could have said hello.

The thought slipped through the cracks, pulsing at the forefront of my mind. There had been plenty of people blocking the front of the saloon, and yet, I'd been able to see his patch clearly. It could have been any of them, but I had known immediately. The broad span of his back emanated the power he wielded. The control as the sea of people parted for him, knowing he wasn't a man they wanted to cross. I should have followed their example. He had no reason to say anything, and there was no expectation that he would single me out. It still hurt, like a pinprick.

I took over my tables, but in the quiet moments, I kept asking myself what the fuck I was thinking. Every interaction I had had with him ended in suspicion. He'd accused me of bringing harm to the town, and I had refused to ease his mind—going in circles until the next time he asked for my story.

Another thought raced forward, but I grabbed my plates, efficiently shutting it down. Putting a smile on my face made it easier to pretend I wasn't overthinking something that didn't exist. Most of the families were gone, shifting into the older clientele that came for lunch after the circus left. They didn't want to wait outside in the heat, and they normally didn't care about seeing a cowboy. It was just a perk. I was dropping a check at a husband and wife's table when the husband stopped me for a quick chat.

"My wife couldn't help watching you. You have such a presence—it's hard to look away. I hope she still looks at me after fifty years." He chuckled.

"She's probably just making sure you don't run off," I said. He reached for his wife's hand, and they both smiled at each other as if they were sharing a private joke.

"Honey," she said to me with a playful glance, "sometimes you've just got to keep an eye on them—make sure they don't get away."

I made a little more small talk before I excused myself, uncomfortable with how close the conversation had come to my thoughts. I should have been numb to being overlooked by now. My mother had never raised me, preferring to tell me I had wrecked her life. She'd bring the latest boyfriend over, trying to keep him happy, so that he'd supply her habit. I'd hidden in the closet, under the bed, anywhere I could be invisible. It had worked, but all it had taught me was the need to hide.

Like mother, like daughter, I hadn't chosen my boyfriends well either. One after another, they'd all been transactional. I would pick one, believing he was my savior, but then I would need something basic and he would turn me away. Each one had shrunk a piece of me until I learned to hold all the pieces close to my chest. I couldn't afford to be hurt, fearing I'd lose myself. It had been one right after another until Jimmy found me. It had been my longest relationship, but the rules were still the same. He'd traded me for his own gain.

Cactus—the protector of everyone but me. He couldn't help it. I recognized the trait ingrained in his core, because no one had ever looked out for me. Maybe this was just a trauma response, and once I left, I'd never look back. Maybe that was the genuine attraction, not to the man, but to the feeling of finally being safe.

It was a lie, and when the older woman had mentioned "not letting him get away," my first thought had been about him. I wanted to believe there was something, but any movement would have to come from him. Cactus would have to find me worthy, and right now, we were a long way away. *Why the fuck do I even care?* I'd sworn off bad boys.

It was my fault. I'd forgotten not to get attached.

Once my car was ready, I'd leave, and no one would remember I had even existed—not even him.

***

"Roxy!" Lulu screamed, waving her hands in my direction as she sat on one of the dining room chairs in Angelica's office. "What the fuck was that?"

"You're asking me? This all started because of you." I shut the door of the office before flopping down in the nearest chair. The night girls had already taken over, and the rest of us were trying to find some energy to go home. It'd been non-stop until five, when the tourists realized there wouldn't be any more possible sightings.

"I thought it was funny when they first told me you were the cowboy whisperer." Francene moaned as she slipped her shoes off. "The people came, so I knew something had happened, but this...I've seen nothing like it."

"We've never made this kind of money in the summer." Angelica laid her head back against her desk chair. "I'd have to check, but I'm not sure we even make this much in winter." She tilted her head, looking at me before she pulled a wad of bills out of her apron pocket. "Before you go, grab this. It's yours."

She'd stepped in to help me, and I really didn't feel like I had earned it. Lulu had taken me outside, but I'd kept up the charade, putting all of us in this strange predicament. "It's okay. Keep it."

"Don't. You earned it." She smiled at me. "If you don't take it, I'll just put it on your books at the garage, like my brother does."

If I hadn't been so tired, I would have put it together quicker. The look on my face must have read the same. The girls started laughing again, but this time, it was at my expense. I wasn't sure I enjoyed being the center of their attention.

"Roxy wouldn't know anything about that, Ang. She hasn't gone to the garage yet, and you know Aces won't call her back." Lulu propped her stockinged feet up on the chair opposite her.

"Seriously? I thought you would have figured it out by now," Ang said directly at me.

"Cactus told me about the money for my car. He said he took the tip money and put it on the books. Brother?" The word felt strange falling off my tongue.

She shrugged. "I haven't talked to him for a few days, so I'm not sure what the status of the repair is."

"Speaking of which, I saw a Saint's Outlaw logo during the circus. They were sneaking out the front door." I added casually as I studied her face for confirmation. Same hair. Same eyes. However, it was more than that. It was in the way they each carried themselves—confident, slightly cocky, and in complete control of the situation. The tilt of their chins when they were right, making the world move around them, not the other way around.

I needed to pull up my big-girl panties and march my ass over to the garage. Depending on the repair, I might leave sooner.

"Yeah, that was him. He popped in for lunch, but when he saw the people with their phones out, he ordered it to go."

All eyes were on me. "I only saw him from the back, so I wasn't sure." I played it off as if I wasn't interested either way, but then it hit me. He had left so that no one would know he was an outlaw biker. "How many people do you think filmed me?" I asked, trying to hide the panic that was rising from my stomach and gripping my throat. It was only a matter of time before the video hit social media, and I needed to be gone.

"You're front and center in every parent's video that filmed their kid."

I'd thrown myself directly into the heart of the circus with no thought of what it might do to me. People knew my name, what I looked like, and where I worked. There was no hiding, even if I was in danger and needed to.

The three of them laughed at what they thought was our good fortune, but once it was serious again, Angelica said the thing no one wanted to admit. "There were cameras, and some parent is going to post that online and tag us. It's inevitable. Whatever this is, it won't stop. I may have to speak to the firm that hires the actors. Right now, they're choosing to eat with us, but if this blows up, we may need to create a schedule to meet customer expectations. It will piss off the other restaurants, but overall, it'll bring in more tourists."

My stomach knotted, and I wanted to run to the restroom, but when they sent up a cheer at the potential money we were going to make, I pretended to go along with it.

Chapter Thirteen

Not Invisible Anymore

Cactus

I sat at the red light, idling my bike on my way to Angelica's. She had some explaining to do about the fiasco that went down the other day. I'd walked into the saloon for a cheeseburger, and half of the room had their cell phones recording. I wasn't dumb enough to think those videos wouldn't land online—throwing all of us into a tilt-a-whirl. It was always what you didn't see coming that did the most damage.

Angelica never spent time at the clubhouse, but anyone—including the tattooed bikers from the other day—could dig up her club connections. I wouldn't let her take a hit for her own success, but she needed to understand how important it was to stay vigilant.

Pulling into her driveway, I parked right next to her SUV. I hadn't been able to talk her out of staying in Tombstone, so I had bought this house, knowing I'd never kick her out. Looking at it now, the house needed fresh paint, and I'd probably have to take care of it this winter to keep the HOA off our asses. Just a bunch of boomers with nothing better to be doing, and since I was on the deed, they liked to jerk my chain. Nothing was amiss in the neighborhood, so at least that was something. The lawns were all manicured in a desert motif, no junk cars, and the sidewalks were clean. The house next door had a realtor sign in the front yard, and when it sold, I'd have to have a chat with the neighbors.

The front door opened, and my sister stood in the entryway. "You coming in or are you going to sit outside all day?" She smiled, happier than I'd seen her in a while. The saloon was doing well for the summer, and I was sure that was one weight lifted off her shoulders.

"Nah, I'm here to rob the place," I teased her. I'd taken Ang to a local store for furniture, but she'd told me no. Said the house was enough, and if someone wanted to rob her, they wouldn't find much. They'd be lucky to find a coffee maker. We'd been joking about it ever since.

"Lasagna's in the oven." She left the door open, heading back towards the kitchen.

I followed her, letting my nose lead my rumbling stomach. "Why don't you serve this on the menu?"

"No one buys it when we do. These are only for emergencies, like today, when I've just had enough."

"Talk to me about the saloon." I didn't give her any room to dance her way out of this, as I sat on a barstool at her counter.

She sat next to me, laying her head against my arm. "I know you saw some of it. The cowboys came in for lunch, and it turned into a cute moment for the kid, but then everyone else wanted the same treatment. There were plenty of parents filming, and the mother of the first kid is some sort of mom influencer. I made Bri look, and she instantly found it. Today, there was a line out the door and down the boardwalk, waiting."

I kissed the top of her head. "I know you're enjoying the success. You've earned it, but anyone who digs into you is going to find secrets that need to stay buried. Your connection to the club. The undercover officer who tried to infiltrate through the saloon. The chick that thought it would be easy to blackmail you."

"I know," she sighed. "The town protects me, but that only goes so far. I'm making a new enemy every time a new customer walks through my door. It creates animosity between the other restaurants."

"Fuck them."

Her head shot up, and she turned in the chair to face me.

"If there's anything new I need to head off, tell me now," I said, making it clear.

"I don't think there's anything new with Lulu, and Francene loves living an uneventful life." Angelica smirked, and my blood ran cold. "You're here because of Roxy. She's front and center in the video they posted, and let's be real, every parent has at least one picture of her."

I scoffed. "We've had this conversation before. She's going to leave. You're going to be hurt. I'll be relieved until the next new person rolls into town."

"The little kid talked to her, and I think she was enjoying the innocence." Angelica placed her hand on my forearm. "When it first started, we tried to tell her, but I don't think she understood. Then with the cameras, and you coming in and getting pickup, she's realizing that she might not be so invisible. It's really rattled her."

"Did she tell you anything I need to know about?" I'd asked her twice, and she'd shut me down both times. If she told Angelica first? I was going to collect on a favor, and I didn't care if she liked it or not.

"No, she likes to fade into the background, like the three of us can't see her. It's such bullshit." Angelica tapped my arm again. "I don't think she's going to hide for much longer. The mom who posted named Roxy. Said her kid couldn't stop talking about the saloon the rest of the day. There were comments about her schedule. One father even said he'd bring his kids back if Roxy waited on them."

Socked feet were heading down the hallway, and small smiles settled on both of our mouths.

"How's that going?" I whispered, waiting for Bri to make an appearance.

"Good, but we've had some serious talks about boys and life. I'm not sure I'm ready for any of this."

"Stop talking about me. I can hear you." My niece turned the corner. The resemblance to Angelica at that age was uncanny. Same face. Same glare. "I'm on house arrest, so it's not like I'm having any fun." She rolled her eyes, opening the refrigerator to get a drink.

"Anyone who is worth your time won't ask you to break the rules. They'll protect you from needing to."

Angelica threw her head back, laughing. "I'll cut you two pieces of lasagna." She pushed up from the stool, heading to the oven. She paused, smirking. "Say hello before you push."

I'd do anything to make sure this didn't fall on Angelica, even if it meant feeding Roxy to the frenzy.

***

Roxy

I barely made it back to the motel. My feet hurt. My head pounded, and I couldn't risk sticking around the saloon to eat—not with the way people were watching my every move. I closed my eyes, willing myself to fall asleep, when there was a light scrape at the door.

Instantly awake, I waited. There were more scraping noises, and the end of a credit card appeared through the doorjamb. I shifted further into the bed. Cactus was breaking in. He was probably here to interrogate me about the viral video. If only I had known. Before, I'd walked from the motel to the saloon and most people left me alone. Now, everyone knew where I worked, and the men with nothing better to do would catcall using my name. As long as they didn't rob me, I could ignore them.

Turning over, I let my back face the door, knowing that it would set Cactus off. It was a favorite pastime of his to tell me how much danger I was in, and I liked to push his buttons, watching the calculated control slip. The door swung on its hinges, and I instantly closed my eyes, pretending to sleep.

The door shut, and I imagined Cactus sitting in the chair that was underneath the desk. I hadn't shoved it below the door handle when I'd walked in earlier. Listening intently, I tried to place where he was in the room, but he startled me when the bed dipped. He must have been sitting behind me.

"You're not sleeping."

I didn't answer, playing the game.

Feeling him lean over my shoulder, he whispered into my ear, "I'm well aware of what you look like sleeping. This ain't it. Don't be a brat."

"Did I earn a spanking, Daddy?" I mumbled, feigning sleep. Part of me speculated whether he'd come closer if I stopped playing pretend.

His hand landed on my ass without warning. I wasn't afraid. He was crude, definitely rude, but he'd pushed none of my boundaries. The heat that rushed up my spine told me I wanted him to.

"Wear jeans and grab a sweatshirt."

"You going to leave me in the desert somewhere they'll never find me?" I made it sound like a joke, but he could make me disappear if he really wanted to, even without a map.

"I'll bring you back to this shitty place."

"It's home sweet home for now," I said, throwing the blankets towards his side of the bed as I stood.

He hissed through his teeth, and I smiled like I hadn't dangled red in front of a bull. I was only wearing a t-shirt and a pair of panties, and while they covered as much as a swimsuit, this was the first time I was showing some skin. Grabbing my jeans, I bent at the hips, dragging them up slow. I could feel the heat of his stare as I reached for my sweatshirt.

"Ready, Daddy."

He looked as if he were in pain.

"Unless you want to stay here." I laughed.

***

Cactus leaned back, his elbows on the blanket he'd spread out before we sat down. He'd brought me to a scenic overlook, the kind the tourists never found. We were out in the middle of nowhere, overlooking miles upon miles of more desert. With the sun setting in brilliant pinks and oranges, it was the most beautiful thing I'd ever seen. I was at peace for the first time in my life, not even minding the company next to me.

"I'll thank Angelica when I see her tomorrow for the lasagna. It was delicious." I swiped at my lips with the napkin before setting my empty plate next to me.

"I stopped by before coming to see you, and she cut two pieces." He stared straight ahead before letting out a deep sigh. "You're not invisible anymore. That's the thanks you get for making a moment for the kid. His mother's video made sure of it. If there's anything you need to tell me about your history, now is the time to do so. I can't protect the saloon if I don't know what to look for."

I should have remembered my place—a part of the saloon. This was an interrogation in disguise.

"Where are you from?" He pretended to watch the sun shift, but he was really studying me from the corner of his eye.

"How long have you been in Tombstone?" I shot back. I didn't expect him to answer, but this week had drained me, and I was angry at myself for making more out of the situation than there was.

"I was in Tombstone for about two years before I went nomad. Came back fourteen years ago and been here ever since." I felt his gaze as he asked me again where I was from.

"The Jersey Shore." I curled my legs in to wrap my arms around my knees. I couldn't get out of telling him something, but I was afraid I would reveal too much.

"It's a long way from there to here, and you don't have the accent." He stacked one boot over the other, swinging them back and forth as he waited.

I said nothing, reminding myself this wasn't about protecting me. This was about minimizing the damage from that mother's video. Lulu had downloaded it and sent it to me. It was cute, but I had been clearly visible. They'd called me by my real name, and there weren't many people named Roxy. If anyone wanted to come find me, they knew exactly where I was.

"My father was career military. Tucson was his last station, but my mother liked to take us to Tombstone for a treat. It was only an hour, and she could wow us as kids with stories about cowboys and bandits. It's probably why I came here when I was eighteen, begging to prospect."

He'd given me a piece of himself. It wasn't anything incriminating, but with how tight-lipped he normally was, I thought this might have been a piece of buried treasure. I laid my chin on my knees, staring off. My story wasn't valuable, but I gave him a piece of me in return. "My mother could barely take care of herself, and I didn't know my father. On the Shore, only the insanely wealthy or the mafia have accents—which is why that's the first thing you notice. We were neither."

The conversation tapered off, each of us staring past the overlook, lost in our own thoughts.

"What is a girl doing driving a car in the middle of the desert?" He'd phrased it openly, so that if I didn't want to tell him, I could work my way out of this conversation, and he would let me. However, I didn't want to hide anything. I wasn't running from the law, and no one was looking for me. If I bypassed the actual answer, I was just as guilty as he made me out to be.

"She dumped her boyfriend at a gas station and took off."

"You running from someone?" he growled.

"No." I could have left it at that, letting him think whatever he wanted. I didn't owe him anything, but I'd had a niggling feeling in the back of my brain, and I needed someone to know, for my safety. "He might see the video and show up. It wasn't an...amicable split."

Silence. Not even the desert dared to whisper.

"Tell me, sweetheart." His voice softened.

I wouldn't hide from my past. Stretching, I moved my plate before turning and crossing my legs to face his profile. "It was Jimmy's bright idea. He sold it as getting out of Jersey, seeing the world, and making more money than we ever dreamed of. I thought it was the stupidest idea I'd ever heard until he wore me down enough to say yes."

He laughed, turning his head towards me. "You really bought that shit? You're smarter than that."

"I'd never been over fifteen miles from the Shore, and like I said, he wore me down. I was having a shit day, and when he brought it up again, it seemed like the answer to starting fresh. North Carolina. South Carolina. Tennessee. I always found work, but he'd always spend it until it was time to go. Usually after a bar fight. I didn't catch on until about Colorado."

His jaw ticked, and his eyes burned into my soul. I knew enough about him to know he wasn't judging me. He couldn't believe I had fallen so long for that gimmick, and truthfully, he was right. I didn't like to think about it because I should have seen the scheme sooner, even though it didn't start out that way.

"Where's Jimmy now?"

"Williams, maybe."

Cactus sat straight up, his whole body turning to face me. "That's Bear Canyon Disciples territory." He shook his head. "What the fuck were you doing there?"

"Working their bar."

His eyes widened, as if he didn't believe me. "I've been in that bar. The brothers get so drunk, they openly fuck the waitresses. Any old lady is fair game as long as you have permission."

"Did you have permission?"

"Didn't want to touch for fear I'd catch something."

"You were probably safer that way." I let out a dry laugh, but it didn't feel funny. "They're not as bad as that, but they get handsy, grabbing anything they can. The night I left, they kept talking about how Jimmy was going to prospect. They couldn't wait because then I'd be fair game."

He muttered something under his breath. It sounded dangerous, even though I didn't understand what he said. Not at me, but for me. I didn't want to know the difference.

"How did you dump him at the gas station?"

I tucked a piece of hair behind my ear before I continued. "I finished my shift, ran to the motel, and grabbed my stuff, but I took an extra minute to breathe. One minute too long, and that's where I fucked up. Jimmy knocked on the window, asking where I was going. I told him I was tired, but I hadn't stopped for gas. He jumped in the car to ride for snacks, and when he left me to head inside, I took off."

"Do you think they're going to come looking for you?"

"I don't know."

We settled back to watch the sun dip down below the horizon. I'd told him everything I thought he should know, but there was still plenty buried beneath the surface. I'd been on the road for a little over a year, and this was the first place I saw myself staying. Building a life for myself that didn't scare me.

When he walked me to my motel door, he stood in the doorway. I didn't know what he was doing, so I asked if he was going to come in.

"Make sure you put the chair underneath the door." He gave me one last look, tapped the door frame and was gone.

Shrugging, I shut the door and placed the chair under the handle. I wasn't invisible anymore, but it would have been nice not to be overlooked.

Chapter Fourteen

Sacrifice the Pawn

Cactus

Throwing my leg over my bike, I pretended I wasn't waiting for her to close her door. The lock clicked loudly, and that was when I finally allowed myself to stare. She'd been right there, leaning against the doorframe, but I'd refused to allow myself to turn around. My feet had felt heavy, like I wore a pair of concrete shoes. She wouldn't have denied me if I had stayed, but the carnage wouldn't have been worth it.

Starting my bike, I revved the engine, peeling out of the parking lot. I didn't have anywhere to go. It was too late to head back to Angelica's. She wouldn't care if I slept on her couch, but she'd ask too many questions I wouldn't answer. I was by myself, and while I could have stopped at some bar, I didn't want to risk breaking some fucking drunk's jaw when he didn't know when to quit.

Driving around, I stuck to the side streets, knowing where I was going but not having any desire to get somewhere. I rode around, but when several pigs went past me with their lights on, I figured my joyriding was over. I didn't need to be caught up in whatever mess they were chasing by myself.

Heading to the clubhouse seemed like my only answer, and while I didn't hate it, I wasn't interested. The main room probably sounded like an orgy, and while I normally banged my fair share, a random fuck had lost its appeal.

The muscles between my shoulders tightened each mile closer to the clubhouse. It settled into my joints, stiffening until I thought they would break. Rolling my neck to release the tension didn't help. I was going to have to suck it up.

Pulling through the main gates reminded me of better times. When I'd been a prospect, this place had felt like home. There had been camaraderie. Now, it felt like every man for himself. Backing my bike into my spot, I took a few deep breaths. It wouldn't do anyone any good if I walked in there ready to fight.

"Where have you been, brother?" It was low and slow—Eights.

I swung my leg over my bike before unclipping my helmet and laying it on my seat. Eights must have been sitting on the porch because he appeared in front of my bike.

"Walk with me," he said, leaving no room for argument.

I fell in step with him, but when he headed towards the fence, I was suspicious. We had cameras in the front near the gate, but we were far enough not to be heard.

Eights turned around and crossed his arms. "You need to know what's going on, and everyone else is busy with their dicks," he drawled. "Seriously, where have you been?"

"Do you know about the video from the other day?" I asked him, not giving anything away I didn't want public knowledge. This was the first time we'd ever talked outside of a few sentences.

"I've seen it." He nodded.

"I was checking on loose ends."

"Yeah, everyone figured that's where you went." Eights puffed out a breath. "I didn't patch in as a Saint to jump down another brother's ass. I won't do that now." He shifted, crossing his arms over his chest. "They were drinking before the girls showed up, you know how it is."

I nodded, wanting Eights to talk faster and knowing I'd have to wait him out.

"Scorpion joked about Roxy, and he didn't let up. By the time the girls came, they were so drunk, they thought it would be hilarious to save you the raven-haired chick for the night. Some brothers figured if you'd walk through the main door, they'd throw her at you. If you turned her down, they'd get their laugh, but truthfully, we're all waiting for you to explode."

"Does this chick know?" I asked, rubbing my eyes, hoping the headache that had been forming would ease for a second. I wasn't in the mood for another one of Scorpion's mind games, knowing I had never given him a reason to send me back on the road. Now, he thought he'd found a weakness with Roxy, and in his mind, he'd exploit her until she cracked. If that happened, I'd snap.

"No. They fed her a line of bullshit, but she's four times Roxy's size. There's no way in fucking hell you're going to take her to your room. She's pretty enough, but your head isn't in it. If you go through the back, no one will know you're here."

My jaw clicked, my back molars gritting hard, which didn't help my headache. "Yeah, I'll take care of it," I said. It was another problem I had to solve, but at least the solution was easy. I was walking off when he reached out and grabbed my arm.

"Is there anything we need to worry about?" He didn't mention the video, but I knew what he was really asking. "Roxy's recognizable if you know her, but the mother tagged the saloon."

"Have you ever been up north? There's a bar in Williams that's Bear Canyon Disciples territory. Mesquite used to be friendly with them," I asked Eights.

"Can't say I've had the pleasure. I was still a prospect, but I've heard most of the stories."

"Roxy worked their bar."

"No fucking shit." Eights blinked hard as his jaw ticked. "I mean, I knew she was tough, but how the fuck did she survive that place?"

"No clue. The first time I went, some club slut was so dirty, I ran. I didn't want to catch anything, so I slept sitting on my bike," I answered honestly. "Roxy's boyfriend prospected with them, and when the president wanted free use, she took off. Landed here."

"Now, the video is going to bring them here," Eights speculated.

"We don't know that, but it could." It was a lie, and we both knew it. I should have put a little faith in him. He'd done me a solid, but I'd become such a lone wolf that I was used to withholding information until necessary. The lie had rolled off my tongue naturally, and I'd never deny it. I said nothing else, but we both knew they were going to come. They would need to make an example of her, and it was only a matter of time.

Eights nodded his head, knowing that I wouldn't give him anything else. "One more thing, and don't shoot the messenger. There's another couple of days' worth of runs. You head out with Tumbleweed tomorrow night."

"You've got to be fucking kidding me." I was furious. I wanted to head into the main room and start swinging, but they'd only take it out on some chick who thought she was going to get lucky. Taking a few deep breaths, I nodded to Eights. He didn't have to stick his ass out on the line.

I'd never asked for anything before, and as I tried to form the words, they stuck to the roof of my mouth. I coughed. Tried again. There was no way I could be in two places at once. "If they show... can you make sure he doesn't throw her into the fire? I won't be here."

"Don't worry about it, brother." He held out his fist for a bump, and I extended mine. I left him standing in the yard, entering the clubhouse from the back. If I had known I was just going to have to hide, I would have stayed at the shitty motel.

Scorpion had the board set. I was the pawn he needed gone. Getting me out of the picture wasn't about safety—it was about hero worship. When it hit the fan, he'd be the one standing in front of Angelica and Bri, holding a shield like he'd bled for this family. Meanwhile, Roxy would bleed as collateral damage. My fists clenched. He wouldn't lose a minute of sleep over it, unless he was fucking some new chick.

It was only a matter of time before the club showed up to claim her, and I wouldn't be there.

***

No one informed me of the three-day run schedule. They had wanted me to find out two seconds before the run left, so that I would scramble to pack a bag. I could have done it, but I didn't want to be the butt of anyone's jokes, especially when this was a test.

Scorpion banged his fist on my door ten minutes before the run was supposed to pull out of the yard, but the joke was on him. I walked out with a packed saddlebag, not saying a word. My middle finger itched, but I refrained from flicking them all off as I strolled towards my bike. They wanted a reaction, but I delivered the punchline when I didn't give them anything.

Tumbleweed was on my left as we drove through the gates, and the select brothers on this run didn't annoy me like some others. It was bad timing, but this could have been worse.

The first run was a repeat cargo security for El Sombra Roja. We met three cargo trucks in the middle of the desert, driving with them to the warehouse near the New Mexico border. No surprises this time, but the cartel didn't schedule cargo deliveries this close together. I suspected El Filo Negro had news for me—the kind he didn't want to deliver over the phone.

The trucks stopped in the middle of the road before they made the turn into the warehouse's driveway. We circled around them, parking our bikes in the paved area that housed visitors. Bike after bike filled the lot, and I waited with the rest of the brothers as the first truck backed up into an overhead door to be unloaded. The other drivers turned off their trucks to wait. As long as they were in the driveway, we were in the clear. No one would challenge the cartel out here, assuming they even knew where to look.

"I hope that one brunette is here," a brother said, smacking his lips.

"It'll take you an hour to get it up, so what good will that do her?" someone else retorted.

I wasn't paying attention to the brothers' antics.

This was our only run for the night before we stayed at a nearby campground. Unloading the three-truck delivery would take the cartel a couple of hours, and afterward, they would expect us to get the fuck out. Until then, we had carte blanche access to the girls upstairs. I'd been up there enough to know why they were excited. El Filo Negro always delivered.

There was a stack of crates near the back wall, and I made my way over there to sit. The brothers were turning the corner of the stairs when I heard loafers clicking on the cement floor behind me.

"Amigo." El Filo Negro perched on the corner of a crate. It was like we'd been here before, neither with good news. We weren't friends, but each faction had its own set of rules that we each respected. There was a difference. "You're not partaking in my gifts again. I'm getting offended."

A laugh bubbled out of my chest, not expecting him to crack a joke. "You're not offended. Whatever those boneheads don't wear out will be more for you and your men later tonight. A man of your position would only feel insulted if I asked you to prospect for the club."

"You're right. I'd get dirty if I had to ride around on a hog all day, amigo. Not my thing. I'd rather get dirty after a workout upstairs."

"How's the pool boy?" I asked, still chuckling. A smirk danced at the corner of my lips.

"Alive. For now. When I get my marching orders, someone will tell my wife." He shrugged. "I'm more concerned about the Lopezes."

We didn't do any business with them, so I wasn't familiar with the name. Shifting on the crate, I crossed my arms over my chest, waiting for him to continue.

"El Sombra Roja has been trying to expand his legit business in America, so he set up an arranged marriage with the Lopez cartel." His hand came up, rubbing at his lip as his foot dangled. "My cousin isn't having a simple time of it, and if she can't produce a child, the marriage falls apart. War is coming."

"You know we won't pick a side." This wasn't our fight, and as long as the money was flowing, we would take our cut and promptly sit this one out.

"The biker gang—they're working with the Lopez cartel to interrupt our cargo lanes."

My poker face remained in place as I processed what he was telling me. It sounded like the biker gang I had asked him to look into had nothing to do with us, but it could all change in a second. If the cartel or those bikers showed up in Tombstone, they would force us into their war. While the club didn't include women, if they wanted revenge, the saloon would be fair game for whomever could hit it first.

Before I could say anything, my phone dinged with an incoming text. I didn't automatically reach for it, in case it was actually club news I needed to hide from the cartel.

"If you head out those doors,"—the Black Blade pointed—"no one will interrupt your conversation. It was good to see you, amigo. I just wish it were under better circumstances." He walked away, heading towards a couple of offices near the back of the warehouse.

Taking his advice, I snuck out the door, walking away from the building until I could barely hear the workers unloading inside. Sweat dripped into my eyes as I pulled out my phone. Wiping the moisture away, I froze.

Eights

We got a visitor at the saloon today.

Chapter Fifteen

The Queen's Gambit

Roxy

I'd survived another day of tourists and their kids begging to see the cowboys. The boys had a staff meeting this morning, but that didn't stop the tourists from whining when no one showed up. A few of the families left disappointed, but Angelica had always made a point of not guaranteeing a sighting. It kept the mystery alive. The two high school girls who worked the evening shift would be here soon. Unless their bus was late, it was no longer my problem.

I was wiping down the tables. The corset was pinching me more than usual today. I couldn't wait to take the uniform off and breathe in nothing but my underwear. Dinner was lukewarm mac and cheese—if the temperamental microwave didn't quit on me first. Sounded like the perfect end to the day.

Bri sighed near the door—the universal sign for boy problems. I buried the chuckle that desperately wanted to escape my chest. Bri was an only child, and while the saloon was close-knit, she didn't have anyone to talk to. I wanted to keep my promise to check in with her, like a pseudo-older-but-definitely-not-wiser sister.

"Hey," I called out to her. She wiggled around the tables, phone still in her hand. "If you want to talk, I'll listen," I threw out there. "Sometimes, it's easier to let go of your troubles with a stranger."

Her eyebrow lifted. Sighing again, she pulled out a chair from the table I'd been wiping down. "There's this boy," she started. Bri looked up at me through her eyelashes. "He wanted me to sneak out last night, but I told him no." Her shoulders sagged, waiting for the lecture she thought I was going to deliver. I'd always chosen the bad boy, and I was the last person to take the moral high ground when I had a cemetery full of regrets.

"Is that him?" I tipped my chin toward her phone.

"Yeah. He won't stop. I told him I wasn't interested anymore if he was just going to make me break curfew."

"You should be proud of yourself. You're seeing the bullshit and calling it what it is. That's more than most girls your age." I smiled, hoping I was delivering something that would empower her. "I was always knee-deep in the wrong guy before I realized I was sinking in quicksand."

"Yeah." She sighed again. "Uncle Grant dished out some advice that made sense. He said boys who don't care if I'm in trouble are not worth my time. The right one wouldn't want to see me hurt."

"That is good advice." My face lifted, surprised.

Bri giggled, watching me. "I refuse to call him Cactus, and I'm cute enough, he lets me get away with it. I bet you could."

I'd heard her, but I pretended I hadn't. I didn't want to know Cactus's real name was Grant. Fuck, I didn't want to think of him as a man. It was easier to see him as a biker, all sharp edges. I could walk away from the biker. Not so much the man. He would demand things I wasn't sure I understood. "Don't settle for what you think is just enough. You deserve better than that."

"You going to settle for my uncle?" Bri giggled again, ignoring her phone as it continued to beep with incoming texts.

I'd spent enough time with Cactus to know he wasn't just someone you settled for. If I let him, he would consume me. Protect me, but not love me. He wasn't capable of love when he used control. I wouldn't break my bad boy rule for the experience, knowing I would leave anyway.

The bell above the door spared me from answering as it dinged, signaling someone walking into the saloon. Bri took off to get them seated, and I breathed a sigh of relief that I wouldn't have to answer her. I didn't want to have to come up with some version of the truth when I was lying to myself.

"Well, aren't you a sweet young thing?"

That voice lived in the back of my brain, degrading me in my weakest moments. Ripper was here, and Bri was too close to him.

The bleach bottle was still in my hand when I shot up, feet already moving. There were eight of them. Ripper, a few of the officers, and in the very back was Jimmy, wearing his prospect cut. *Coward.* At one time, I'd thought he was my forever. Watching him now, all I felt was fury.

Ripper raised his hand—slow, deliberate.

My stomach churned. "Don't touch her," I yelled, hoping Angelica would hear me from the back.

Bri backed up, but she didn't have very far to go before she bumped into the nearest table.

"Well, lookie what the cat dragged out. Roxy." Ripper was exactly as I remembered him. His dirty-blonde hair looked like it hadn't been washed for days. A white shirt, almost gray, stretched tightly across his beer belly. His natural, repugnant scent would fill my nose if I got too close.

I put Bri behind my back, holding the spray bottle like a dangerous weapon. If it came to it, I'd blind him, taking my chances. "This is Saint's Outlaws' territory." I was bluffing, but Ripper wouldn't know any different. I wanted to put fear into him.

"Yeah, but you're my property, and we've come to collect."

"It'll be a cold day in hell before I leave with you voluntarily." I tapped Bri's leg, still holding the bottle. I needed her to send a text for reinforcements. The only way to get Ripper to see straight was to call the Saints. They'd have some alpha chest-bumping brawl, and I'd sneak out the back. No goodbyes as I ran.

He took a step closer, and I sprayed the bleach mixture on his shirt. "You need to leave. The town instantly clocks outsiders."

"She's right." Angelica walked into the dining room from the kitchen. "If you're hungry, you're more than welcome to eat before you leave." She moved to pull a few tables together, like this was a regular rush.

"I'll help her," I whispered to Bri. "Why don't you go get the menus?" We both knew the menus weren't in the kitchen, but if I could get Bri out of here, then I'd take all the hits. Angelica and I locked eyes. This was bad, and I'd brought trouble to her door. *Just like Cactus warned.* He'd seen the storm coming.

"Gentlemen, if you're staying for lunch, we have your table ready." Angelica waved her arm over the two she'd stuck together. She was always in control, and this was no exception, but I was hoping I'd see just a tiny break. Something that would make me feel human. I was trying not to freak the fuck out, but it was taking an enormous effort not to shake.

"I've never been interested in mamas and their babies, but you could change my mind," Ripper chuckled as he sat at the head of the table. The rest of the idiots made nuisances of themselves, cackling like old ladies. Ironically, Jimmy was the only one who didn't laugh.

"I don't suggest you say that again. The only thing on the menu is the food." She nodded toward where we kept a stack of menus, and I took the hint. If we pretended they were customers, we might buy enough time until the Saints arrived. There was no way Angelica hadn't called Scorpion already. If not, then Bri surely would have texted her father.

"Can I get you anything to drink? We have water and soda: regular, diet—"

"I don't fucking want soda." Slick, the treasurer, threw his knife into the wall. It stuck in the wood slats of the saloon, sticking straight out.

"That won't scare me, but if you continue to make asses of yourselves, I will include a redecorating fee. Pick a drink." Angelica didn't show an ounce of weakness, her tone slicing through their childish antics. She was standing far enough from the table that none of them could reach out and grab her.

"How about I get you to slurp my dick down?"

Angelica said nothing as she raised the bar gate, sliding underneath. She picked up the soda gun, clicking a switch. I watched her shoot soda all over Slick, not stopping until the gun sputtered empty. "You needed a cooldown."

"You bitch!" He charged toward her, but she stood her ground, clicking another button of the soda gun and holding it up. He didn't stop, reaching for her, but she fired, nailing him in the face with red juice.

"We serve that to good boys when their parents say it's okay."

Crank, the enforcer, stood, flipping the table behind him. He threw the chair against the wall, and we all watched as splintered pieces flew around the room.

I stared in horror as more chairs met the walls of destruction. There was nothing I could do that wouldn't draw attention to myself. I picked my brain for any sliver of an idea, but I couldn't come up with anything under pressure.

I'd forgotten the rest of the bikers in the room as Ripper started laughing hysterically. He'd stood from his chair and was heading directly toward me. He advanced, but I kept taking steps backward to keep the distance between us. "Jimmy, you wouldn't deny your president, would you?" he cackled.

"No, sir." Any love I felt for Jimmy died a slow, painful death. He was weak, and this had proven it.

"You won't get close enough to touch me." I took another step, but I hit the front of the back bar. It only caused Ripper to laugh some more. He placed his hands on either side of me, grabbing the bar before he leaned down, smelling me. I froze at the intrusion into my personal space.

His body odor invaded my nose, waking me up. "This is Saint's Outlaws territory. You need to leave before you can't come back from this," I whispered.

"Fuck the Saints." He leaned forward, running his nose underneath my ear. His breath smelled of old coffee. I didn't fight. Instead, I brought my knee up, planning on driving it hard into his dick. He predicted the move, grabbing my leg to hold me in place, pushing his dick against me. "See, I always knew you wanted me."

I gave in, freezing as I listened to the sounds of the saloon being destroyed. This was my fault. I deserved this, I thought, swallowing. I tuned out. The sounds faded into a buzz between my ears.

No, I won't give in. Not today.

I nuzzled his neck with my nose, giving him a false sense of security. He moaned, and my stomach wanted to revolt violently. I trampled it down as I moved to suckle his earlobe. This was only a distraction, and I needed to keep focused on what mattered—safety and the saloon.

"We'd be good together, Rox," he moaned.

It was all the encouragement I needed. I wouldn't allow myself to get caught in whatever game this was. He didn't own me. My teeth clamped down, but when he pulled away, I held on tighter. The earlobe tore. I had actually done it. As the adrenaline kicked in, my hands shook. Clenching them into fists, I didn't let anyone see me fall apart. I would later.

"Well, fuck me sideways."

Scorpion.

The Saints were here.

Chapter Sixteen

Checkmate

Roxy

Each time Ripper moved his head, the hanging skin flapped. I'd never known a biker to be squeamish about blood, but every time he brought his dirty hand up to poke it, he'd double over, making retching sounds. I said nothing, preparing to run if he actually threw up. He needed to man up. I had a pool of blood in my mouth, and I hadn't moved away from the bar.

"You fucking bitch," he spat. I still said nothing, reaching for a napkin to wipe the spittle off my face, but he was quicker. His hand cracked against my cheek, sending me to the ground, but I grabbed the bar, digging my nails into the wood. I wouldn't lay at this asshole's fucking feet. It took me a minute to bounce back, but he just laughed at me. I wasn't a weak little girl. He was just a dirty bastard. I pulled back, spitting the glob of blood into his face.

"You should have left when you had the chance." I smiled, hoping I still had blood on my teeth. I wasn't a fan of other people's blood, but at least I wasn't gagging. Ripper reached back to hit me again but hesitated when Scorpion's voice rang out across the room.

"Hit her again, and I'll use your head to clean up this floor."

Ripper wrapped his sweaty hand around my bicep, thinking we were going to leave the saloon. "We got what we came for, so we'll be leaving now," he called to his men, but no one moved.

Scorpion stepped in front of him mid-stride. "You're not going anywhere. Let go of her." Each syllable was drawn out.

Scorpion wasn't high on my list, but I wouldn't let him see me flinch. He wasn't here to protect me, but I didn't fear him. If he kicked me out of the saloon after this, he wouldn't do it until after they left. There were worse things in life than death, and at least Scorpion would make it quick, taking me out into the desert.

The only person who could protect me from Scorpion's wrath was Cactus. I scanned the room, checking each face. Too young. Too heavy. Definitely too skinny. He wasn't here, and my heart sank. It was my fault, letting him take up space in my mind. He was someone I barely knew. Giving him power over my fear was my fault. I wouldn't make that mistake again.

"I've been to your shithole of a bar, so I'll understand if this is like culture shock. You're going to get a beatdown for this, so why not make it easier on yourself?" Scorpion shot me a look over Ripper's shoulder. A silent message to fight the hold.

I had been dead weight he was dragging behind him, so when I squirmed, banging my free fist against the patch on his back, he couldn't maintain his grip on my arm. Letting me go, he was stuck facing Scorpion. A slow, cruel smile stretched across his face before he balled his fist, smashing it into Ripper's face. He followed it up with several hits to Ripper's chest and gut, like it cost him nothing.

Ripper doubled over, holding his stomach in. "Enough."

"This is only the beginning." His eyes went to Angelica's, still standing behind the bar with the soda gun in her hand. Before he could say anything, the front door opened. Aces strolled in with one of the other Saints. I recognized him from that lunch, but no one had introduced us.

"All taken care of. Sheriff can't wait to collect $500 a bike." Aces laughed, the sound hollow as he surveyed the room.

"Don't forget our tow fee," the other brother chuckled.

"Sucks to be you, bitches. Are we at the beatdown yet? I need to release some tension." Aces jumped up to sit at the end of the bar, swinging his feet and cracking his knuckles.

"What the fuck did you do to our bikes?" one of the Disciples brothers growled.

It didn't surprise me they were more concerned about their bikes. They had the prospects wash them more often than the brothers actually bathed.

"It's now past five, and you're not patronizing a business, so the sheriff had you towed from the visitors' lot. Unfortunately, you'll have to camp in the desert because the office will be closed by the time you get out of here." A snicker from the Saints floated around the room.

In my experience, most bikers gave off a dangerous air, but I hadn't been afraid. Once I gave the impression I wasn't interested, they left me alone. It wasn't until Williams that it changed. The Bear Canyon Disciples were dangerous men, but they often used their numbers to bully their way, and I was now their focus. However, the Saints made them look like chumps.

Scorpion grabbed a chunk of Ripper's hair, forcing him to stand. "There's a clause in the paperwork that says we're not responsible for any damage that occurred during the tow, so when you find that big scratch in your paint, no, you didn't."

He let him go, kicking him in the stomach on the way down. "Here's how this is going to go, so you fucks better listen up," he addressed the room, getting distracted when his eyes scanned over to Angelica behind the bar. Marching through the soda on the floor, he stood in front of her. "Butterfly, don't even think about it." He smirked.

"I'm going to have to close tomorrow, thanks to these fuckwits." She swiped one of her bangs away from her eyes.

"You know I'm going to take care of it." He patted her cheek, but her eyes were still blazing. "Trust me."

"Fuck you." She raised the soda gun level with his chest as she flicked the button.

"Is the kitchen cleaned up?" He ignored her, letting his hand caress the apple of her cheek.

She shook her head. The cooks had been switching over from lunch to dinner when the club had stormed through the front door.

"You're done here. Take the staff out back. They've got the day off tomorrow—with pay."

She started to argue but stopped herself. Nothing she would say would change any of this.

"No, I'll take care of it. Go." He patted her cheek again before prying the soda gun from her hand. Laying it on the bar, he held her hand, lacing their fingers together as he led her towards the bar gate. Picking it up, he let her walk in front of him with her head held high.

I met her in the middle of the dining room, holding out my hand. She locked our fingers together, giving me some of her strength, but when we passed Slick, lying on the floor, she stopped. Pulling her leg back, she landed a kick to his stomach before we made our way to the back of the dining room. It didn't do any damage, but I swore I saw a smirk on her lips.

When the kitchen door closed behind us, the sounds of a fight floated through the crack in the door. I could only guess how much damage Angelica was going to incur—all because I had been nice to a kid.

"I'm sorry," I whispered. This was all my fault. I'd put it off long enough. I needed to go check on my car so that nothing like this would happen again. Angelica had given me an opportunity, and I had repaid her with blood on the walls and broken furniture.

"Don't fucking say that. You didn't know they were going to behave like Neanderthals." She hugged Bri before ushering us out the back door of the saloon. "At least one good thing happened today." She smiled. "I'm getting the renovations I've been hounding Scorpion for."

"Dad doesn't always keep promises," Bri whispered, but Angelica ignored it.

If I had stayed forgettable, none of this would have ever happened.

***

Cactus

Eights had said nothing else, and I didn't bother texting him back. I wasn't interested in hearing what had happened from him. If I asked, he would tell me, but I wanted to hear it from her. The need to call her rode my ass as we sat down in the warehouse for dinner.

The brothers took their sweet time eating, and I would have offended our hosts if I rushed them. I tried to make enough small talk not to be noticed, but the girls had picked their favorites. They sat on laps, trying to feed the brothers for attention. It wasn't until I caught the back of a head with short raven hair, nuzzling the neck of a brother, that I had to bury my anger. It wasn't her, but that need cranked up another notch.

We headed out with our payment a couple hours later, driving down toward the Mexican border. Another hour of pretending the open road fixed everything. Tomorrow wouldn't be any different. Just another wasted day, burning gas and pretending I gave a shit. I'd end up doing this all over when Scorpion found another excuse.

I was rolling out my sleeping bag inside one of the pop-up tents we rented when a shadow crossed over me. "Can I help you?" I snapped, looking over my shoulder. Cowboy boots—Tumbleweed. He was the only brother who refused to wear regular shitkickers.

"Hey, brother." He squatted next to me, his arm brushing mine as he laid it on his thigh. "Is she alright?"

"How would I know?" I asked him. I pushed him over in the dirt, but he just popped back up into a squat. Tumbleweed was resilient. It didn't matter how many times he got steamrolled. Fucker always stood up. "How do you know?"

"You didn't answer Eights, so he wanted to know if you were alright."

"Tell him to go fuck himself." I didn't want him to think we were friends.

"If you find a dark corner, I won't come looking for you." Tumbleweed whistled, standing up before strolling back to his tent on the other side of the fire. The brothers were in small groups, roaming around the campsite. They were busy having a good time, but they knew better than to drag me into it. They lied so much they'd forgotten the truth.

Prick, I thought, which instantly reminded me of *Roxy. What the fuck would I even say to her? She'd think the call was mainly about what happened and not her.*

I shoved the end of my sleeping bag in, closing the tent. Sticking close to the edge of the dark campsites, I stopped when I was three away from ours. No one could sneak up on me.

Sitting on a log around the darkened fire pit, I dialed her phone number from memory. She'd filled her employee paperwork with her actual information, and I'd stolen her phone number right before we'd left.

The phone rang before clicking over to her voicemail. I called again—nothing. She didn't have the burner phone's number. After the day she had, I didn't blame her for not answering a strange number.

Hitting the phone against my leg, I wanted to throw it across the unlit firepit. Caving, I sent her a text.

(520) 589-0819

Call me back, sweetheart.

I waited. I'd give her ten minutes before I tried another round of calls. It hadn't even been a minute when my phone rang with an incoming video call. Did I answer? It wasn't like I hadn't had video calls, but I didn't want to reveal anything that would put a target on her back.

You're sitting at an empty campsite. Answer the call. I hit the green button, waiting until her face appeared in the screen. She was lying in bed, the ugly motel walls behind her. The exhaustion was clear on her face as she curled under the covers.

"I can't see you," she said, adjusting the phone she must've propped up.

I turned my phone's flashlight on.

"Hi," she said, laying back down on her pillows.

"Hey, how are you?" My hand came up to palm my face at how stupid I sounded. I was lucky, catching it before she could see the motion in the camera.

"Fine."

"Roxy, you're not fine. Why don't you tell me what happened?" I held my phone in one hand, tracing the dark shadows under her eyes on the screen. She looked worn out—the kind of tired that made people do dumb shit out of fear.

She huffed a few times before the entire story came out in quick bursts, not bothering to breathe in between. "When we walked out the back door, the bar melee had just started. I came here, and that's it."

"They'll be gone before I get back, but this was an opportunity for Scorpion to play hero. He'll make sure they're reminded to call first before they show up at our doorstep next time."

"Yeah, but Angelica took me in when she didn't have to, and now, the saloon can't open until the renovations are done. I caused that. I'm going to pop over there tomorrow to see if they need a hand and check on my car."

"You're determined to be a martyr for this, but all you did was give those guys a chance to fight. Now, they'll be good for at least a few days. Angelica's been asking for some updates, so don't worry about it. Plus, if you try to apologize, she'll just wave it off."

"Would you have fought?" Her eyes blazed through the screen. Subconsciously, she wanted reassurance that she belonged.

"I would have." I'd never sat out a fight as long as I was here.

"For me or as a Saint?" she pushed.

"Hey, I should let you sleep. We'll talk tomorrow." I was running as if I were doing Mach 5. I couldn't give her the answer she wanted, probably because I had never stopped to consider she could be mine.

"Right." There was a hiccup in her tone, and that was when I realized she wasn't angry. She was done.

The screen went black in my hand.

Fuck. I'd royally fucked up. I could have said yes. Instead, I'd let her believe she was just another woman I was trying to conquer.

I thought about calling her back, making her talk to me until she fell asleep on her own. I had two more days on the road, and every nerve was screaming at me to fix it. Hovering over the green button, I stopped right as my thumb came close enough to hit it.

If there was a chance to make amends, I was going to have to do it in person.

Chapter Seventeen

Don't Quit Your Day Job

Roxy

The sun blinded me as I stepped out of my motel room. I didn't have sunglasses, so I quickly locked my door and headed downstairs to the parking lot. I hadn't been able to sleep, tossing and turning all night until I had just given up—worrying about the saloon and what the fuck Cactus's problem was.

Ignoring the urge to check my phone, I stopped on the sidewalk, tilting my head back to soak in the sun. I wasn't his keeper, and if he texted, I'd answer when I had a free moment. A catcall came from somewhere behind me. *Of course. Perfect timing, assholes.* It was a good reminder that I couldn't depend on a man.

Nothing good could come from trying to figure out last night. I was an outsider, and once I was gone, he wouldn't have to worry about how I was going to disrupt their quiet lives. I'd been a fool. Whatever shift I thought was happening was just a figment of my imagination.

My phone beeped, begging to be checked, but I shoved the urge down deep. I wouldn't get giddy over a good-morning text. If he asked me how I was, I would respond cordially. It was a little girl's fairytale dream to have her knight come to her rescue. I had taken a small leap of faith when I had asked about the fight, but when he couldn't answer, that had sealed my fate. I wouldn't ask again.

As I opened the back door to the saloon, my phone vibrated against my ass. Ignoring it, I called out into the kitchen. The stainless-steel countertops shone under the lights. The kitchen staff always kept things clean, but this was something else. Sticking my head in between the two prep rows, I checked to make sure I had missed no one.

Pushing open the swinging door that blocked the kitchen from the dining room, I called out again.

"There she is," Aces sang. He was sitting on the bar, dangling his legs over the edge.

"No one wants to eat where your ass has been," I said.

No one would have ever known there had been a bar fight here last night. Someone had painted the walls in the dining room a fresh hunter green, bold against the polished trim. The bar shone, and I didn't see any sticky residue. In fact, it sparkled in the light as if someone had added a couple of coats of varnish.

The splintered furniture was gone, but nothing new had replaced it. The surviving tables and chairs stood against the far wall. I wasn't sure if we had enough to fill the dining room for service.

"They had to order new ones. They'll be here later this afternoon, which is why we're hanging out." Eights was sitting in the chair closest to where I stood. The rest of the Saints were situated around the room. Some played on their phones, while others napped.

I nodded at Eights, before leaning against the bar, biting back what I really wanted to say. "Did you work all night?" I asked Aces.

"Yeah. Had to make sure none of you had anything to bitch about." He flexed a few times, like he had done all the work himself.

"Don't listen to him. We hired a cleaning crew. They did most of this, but it was a late night." Eights came up behind me. "How are you?"

"Okay." I kept my head up, shoulders back. "Is there anything I should do?"

"Nope." Aces' legs swung, and I wanted to put my hand on his knee to stop them. I didn't, knowing he'd get the wrong idea.

"Have you started working on my car? I've been trying to call, but you must be busy, since you never answer."

"Nope, I've been ignoring you."

I tried to keep my cool, but I really wanted to yell and scream at him. "Why would you do that?"

"You've got a crack in your radiator, and I don't have the part. That's not very customer-friendly." He shrugged. "Besides, I can't get yelled at for telling you something you don't want to hear if I don't tell you at all."

"Do you know how much it's going to be?" I tried to convince myself it wouldn't be expensive.

"You shouldn't quit your day job, but you could pay it off another way."

I watched a smirk form on his lips. It didn't click until he made a hand motion at Eights behind me. I'd rather stay in town than pay on my knees. It wasn't even funny, and when I caught the look on Eights's face behind me, he clearly didn't think it was amusing either.

"You're disgusting. You sure you shouldn't have ridden out with the Disciples? They'd be just your type." I started to walk away before turning around to face them again. "Besides, I prefer to be in charge."

The front door opened, and Lulu walked in with fancy coffees, ending the conversation.

***

A supplier had already delivered the glassware, and the boxes were lined up in front of the bar. I desperately wanted to be helpful, opening the flap of the top box—salt and pepper shakers.

"Hey," I asked the nearest brother to me. I'd never seen him before, and none of them had introduced themselves when I'd walked in earlier. "How much damage can salt and pepper shakers do?"

"You'd be surprised." He grabbed one from the box. "There's enough glass that if you aim well and throw hard enough, the cuts sting like a bitch." He shrugged. "All the glass was on the floor, so it was easier to order everything new."

I could only imagine how much this was costing Angelica. I had to remind myself there was nothing I could have done to prevent this, but I couldn't hold the sadness back, staring at the breakables.

"Grab a box or two, and I'll go grab the refill containers. No one bothers the help." Lulu winked at me, running past. We were both pretending all of this was normal, when we should have been slinging hamburgers and fries.

It was easier to be busy than to stop and worry about what was going to come next. Lulu must have been thinking the same thing because we made small talk at one of the older tables as we worked, but it was nothing like the jokes we normally cracked. I wasn't sure how long we'd been at it. I was deep in thought, trying to decide what to do next.

"You've got that look," Lulu said as she poured pepper into a shaker.

I didn't bother responding. If I told her the truth, she'd only try to talk me out of it. She wanted to keep me, and while I enjoyed her company, this wasn't my home. My phone beeped, but I continued dumping salt into my shaker.

"Are you going to check that?" she asked me, with a small smile.

"Nope." I didn't need to check it to know it was Cactus. The brothers' reactions gave it away. Each time my phone dinged with an incoming message, they would point and giggle. I would ignore it, but one of them would text him back. I could only guess what they were telling him. They were busy having fun, but to the rest of us that actually worked here, this was too sad for words.

"What happened, sweets?"

Something in Lulu's tone made me pick up my head to look at her. Her lips curved into a sad smile, as if she had been in my position too many times.

I searched the room, scanning to see if any of the brothers were paying attention to us. I didn't need them up my ass. They would tease me, and I wouldn't have any recourse to make them stop. They'd also tell Cactus, and while he might not care, he was prickly. It could go either way, but I could only see him starting a fight. "I fucked up," I whispered. "I made a mountain out of a molehill."

"A mountain..." Lulu cracked up, laying her head against the back of the chair. "Where the fuck did you get that expression?" I'd never heard Lulu swear, but it wasn't hard to pick up when the brothers were loud.

"Somewhere in the Midwest." I chuckled, watching the genuine enjoyment on her face. Lulu smiled often, but I had noticed it hardly reached her eyes. I wasn't sure if I was the only one who recognized she hid pain. "Cactus called last night."

"Oh." Her lips made an O shape as she dragged out the syllable. "Did you ask where you stood? There's nothing wrong with that, sweets."

"Yeah, but now I'm ignoring him. He told me to 'get some rest,' like I'm a little kid he has to take care of." *I had just wanted someone to pick me for once.*

"Girl! You should have told me. I would have helped you string him along until he couldn't see straight. Oh, my God."

Aces heard the end of her diatribe when he straddled one of the remaining chairs at our table. "You rang?" He smirked.

"No one called you." She ignored him, turning back towards me. "We should have a girls' night." Lulu bounced back quickly.

"You're the one who wanted an invitation to my bed."

"Shouldn't you be unloading the tables, or something?" Lulu reached for the pepper container, but he grabbed it before she could. "What I said was there were plenty of prospects if you would just ask." She rolled her eyes.

"What's wrong with you people?" I chimed in. "You run your mouths, talk a good game, and when it comes down to it, you have the emotional awareness of a gnat."

"Have to have water for gnats." Aces shrugged, crossing his arms over the top of the chair. "Read those texts yet?"

"Fix my car yet?"

His jaw dropped as if I had sucker-punched him. His gaze slid over the dining room until it landed on where Eights was carrying in one of the new chairs. "Hey

Eights, you tell Cactus his bitch is as prickly as he is?" Laughing, he stood before I threw a salt shaker at him.

"No one's bitch," I yelled at Aces's back, and I swore Lulu's hand reached for one of the pepper shakers. We were on the same page.

"Yeah, we're too much for you to handle," Lulu chimed in.

"I sent him a proof of life picture." Eights lingered on Lulu a beat too long. "He's going to owe me," Eights muttered, more to himself. She didn't look impressed, so I didn't pretend to be.

The rest of the brothers had stopped what they were doing to watch this exchange. They couldn't contain their laughter, and it bounced off the rafters.

"Fuckers," I whispered, sliding towards the back of my chair.

"Do you have club clothes?" Lulu whispered to me. "We'll grab Angelica and go dancing tomorrow night. If we pick up a few cowboys, more power to us. They need to remember who we are. There are plenty of men who'd be grateful for our attention. Fuck them."

Fuck them. I didn't bother checking my phone, deleting his messages without opening them. It was going to be a while before my car was ready. I didn't have enough money to buy a new one, so I'd have to wait, but I could avoid him. I'd done all right before things had become serious.

Once my car was ready, I'd leave. I didn't need him to pick me. I'd picked myself. Dancing sounded fun. Fuck him.

Chapter Eighteen

Other Fish In The Pond

Roxy

"Did you warn her about this place?" Angelica asked Lulu, sitting in the passenger seat. "The news said a girl went missing out the back last week, but they didn't say if anyone found her." She shifted, crossing her ankles.

"I left a few things out." Lulu drew out the syllables. "If I had told her all the stories, she'd have said no. We're safe if we stick to the rules." Lulu sighed. "It's not like we have time to do a real girl's weekend in Phoenix."

"The last time we were here, the boys got into a fight with some of the local cowboys. When they called the police, the sheriff specifically showed up and detained all of us. He only knows the basics, so he thought we would rat them out."

I watched Angelica sift through her purse until she found her wallet. I watched as she slid her license through the plastic window and grabbed some cash, folding everything tight. It was all I needed to see to know exactly what type of place we were heading to—the kind where desperate women did stupid things.

I should have said something, demanding they take me back to my motel, but I didn't. I'd been sixteen the first time I'd run and hid in a place that sounded eerily similar. It had been a warehouse, converted into a club, where no one gave two fucks what you wore. As long as I hadn't tried to order an alcoholic drink, the bouncers had left me alone. It had been my sanctuary, safer than being at home with my mother and her then drug-dealing boyfriend.

I said nothing, knowing I could handle whatever this place offered but not comfortable at the idea of relieving a past I'd thought I'd put behind me.

Lulu killed the engine before they both leaned over the center console to peer at me. "Ground rules," Lulu said, smiling wide. "Leave your phone here. You'll never notice it's gone until you get a ransom note from across the border. Don't ask me how I know." She palmed her face, shaking her head.

"No purse. Put your money and your license in your bra," Angelica chimed in.

"We go in pairs to the restroom. No exception." Lulu pointed her finger at me, as if I was the one who would get them killed.

Angelica turned her head to face Lulu. "Did we forget anything?"

"I don't think so." Lulu faced me again. "Questions?"

"Why are we doing this again? It doesn't sound fun." Lulu had sold tonight as a girl's trip without leaving town. Dancing, drinking, and flirting. If she had told me there were rules, I wasn't sure I would have agreed.

It wasn't about being afraid. I'd been to plenty of places with rules—biker bars, clubs, and underground raves. They all had the same edge of danger. Rules didn't instantly mean something to fear. They were more about survival, and I was tired of constantly dodging the sinkholes looking to swallow me whole. I wanted more, something for myself without the scars and the warnings. I didn't know if there was a future like that for someone like me.

"To remind ourselves there are other fish in the sea." Lulu meant well, but she was trying too hard to forget she was still swimming in the same pond. "They might even come with less bullshit."

New prospects didn't excite me. Men required work, and I wasn't interested in playing emotional interpreter just to make them feel like men. More rules, and if I wasn't perturbed at Lulu, I might have found humor in the irony.

Don't flirt too hard, but make sure they feel attractive.

Don't oversell yourself.

Dress to impress, but not like you need attention.

Jimmy was in the past. After he had sat in the saloon playing yes-man to Ripper, any respect I'd had for him had died a slow, painful death. He wasn't a man, but I didn't have the heart to autopsy two years of bad choices. They were there, waiting for me to close the door.

The future didn't seem so bright either, as I realized I had fallen into the same trap. I'd accepted scraps for so long, I thought that was what I deserved. Cactus would show up for a few hours, and even though nothing had happened, I was fine accepting whatever energy he had left. It wasn't enough. I wanted to be first in my man's life, and Cactus didn't have room for one more.

He was the Sergeant at Arms, and the club would always come first. If he wasn't running to do their bidding, then Angelica and Bri were next. I wasn't angry about that, and I didn't resent his family. It was just the way it was.

I hadn't heard from him. Someone must have leaked that I had deleted the text messages the morning we cleaned up the saloon. He'd taken my silence seriously.

Lulu opened her door and stepped out of the car. We heard her huff before she leaned down. "Aces will pick me one day." She hesitated for a second. "Doesn't mean I'll say yes." She nodded at Angelica. "When was the last time you had a real date?" She then looked at me over the headrest. "You ghosted, so now what?"

"Aces is too much of an asshole to be a real dom. If you're looking for someone who might actually want to fulfill your needs, we could always find a dungeon or something." I threw the idea out there, knowing the men would hate it if they heard us. "Think about it. You walk in, you tell some hot dom what you want, and they actually do it. No ego-stroking bullshit needed, or so I've heard."

"Do those exist?" Angelica's eyes widened, highly considering the field trip.

"Yeah, and the ropes come with fewer strings attached."

Lulu ignored us as she slammed her car door shut.

"Might as well get this over with." Angelica shrugged as we exited the car.

My nose wrinkled the second I saw the place. It looked like a barn someone had tried to pass off as a club. Nothing but dark corners and too many exits. I got the rules. The parking lot was in the front, and I could see the bouncers standing near the door. However, if you walked around the sides, you could easily disappear into the desert landscape.

"Ladies," the bouncer said as we approached. He opened the door, not bothering to check our IDs. "Don't think about taking a souvenir home."

Angelica smirked before patting the bouncer on the cheek. "You didn't patch in, so don't think you get to threaten me." She wiped her hand on the sleeve of his shirt and then swatted the air, as if he were beneath her. She'd effectively dismissed him, walking through the door like she owned the place.

The music thrummed through the floor, vibrating off the walls, only to fade into the rafters. At least they were playing something I recognized. Darkness settled in every available space until the circulating spotlights hit. There were people everywhere, and I was ready to go home. Plastering a smile on my face, I yelled at the other girls, "We should get a drink!"

We squeezed our way to the front, waiting for a bartender. I was leaning against the bar, watching the dancefloor, when I heard a giggle next to me. *Angelica could giggle? Maybe this was* the *attention she didn't get from Scorpion.* My head slowly turned to the left. Tucking a piece of hair behind her ear, she smiled at whatever the bartender had said.

"He's cute," I whispered in her ear as he popped off the beer caps.

"Fun for right now," she said, "and probably age-appropriate."

"If you're going to take him for a test drive in the bathroom, you have to have a chaperone." I nudged her with my elbow before grabbing my beer. "I'm going to dance." She nodded, as if she had heard me, shooing me away. Lulu was on my other side, chumming it up with some frat boy. "Want to dance?" I asked her.

The conversation must not have been that exciting because she grabbed her bottle, took one look at Angelica, and followed me. We found a spot near the edge where some of the other girl groups were. There was a bachelorette party going on, and they all wore pink sashes. Waving their hands, they screamed for us to join them, but we waved them off. They were attracting too much attention, and I was still looking only to have fun.

A country song blared from the speakers when Lulu put her hand on my hip, drawing my focus to her. She pressed against my back, but I thought nothing of it. This was Lulu. "You have an admirer," she whispered in my ear.

Pulling away, we danced, bumping hips and grinding against legs, and anything else we could reach. For someone who wanted to go fishing, Lulu showed more interest in me than she did the men in the room.

"Can I borrow her?"

"You make her uncomfortable, I'll break your face." Lulu's voice snapped me out of my daze.

"That's fair, Lulu." A man grabbed my hand, turning me around until I faced his chest. There was a slow song playing, and he gathered me against him. I should have fought or tried to pull away, but it was too smooth. My only choice was to follow along.

His eyes were familiar, a chocolate brown that I couldn't place. I scanned his face for something identifiable. No broken nose or crooked smile, and when I tried to sniff discreetly, nothing. I was drawing a blank, but he'd called Lulu by name.

"Draw a mustache on me," he said, chuckling in my ear. He was clean-shaven, and when I squinted, I still couldn't picture where I knew him from. "Miss Roxy, I'm very disappointed. I thought we had something."

Doc. *The re-enactor was here.* Dancing. *With me.* Of all nights. "You're fake... It's fake." I was talking about the mustache, but nothing was coming out right.

"It gets glued on in the morning." He was still chuckling at me as we made another turn.

"You should grow one. Unless you can't." The words tumbled from my lips, unfiltered. Mortified, I wanted the dance floor to open up and swallow me whole.

A smirk slowly appeared on his lips before he tilted his head back, laughing. He didn't criticize me. Nor did he mock me to see if he could hurt me. I'd never been in a relationship with laughter, and I was seeing its appeal. I couldn't help but think that if I found a man like Doc, it would make my life simpler. Comfortable.

Except I'd always chosen the dark, not to be seen as long as I stayed out of the spotlight.

"I can grow one," he said, still trying to catch his breath. "It just doesn't look as nice as the one the city buys. I'm Kevin."

"I'll never call you Kevin, Doc."

We danced a few songs before I looked for Lulu, feeling like I had abandoned her. Doc found her in the crowd before I did, pointing to where she danced with the actor who played Morgan Earp. It made me feel better, and every time we checked on Angelica, she was fine. She hadn't moved from her spot at the bar.

Song after song played until my head spun. I wasn't sure how I was still on my feet. I was dancing, if you could call it that, when Doc put his arm around my back and pulled me close. "Want to tell me why a Saint's Outlaw is staring at you?"

"Handlebar mustache?" I didn't need the confirmation. Cactus was here. My stomach dropped, and I almost took off running for the bathroom without a chaperone.

"Yeah, and it twirls at the ends." Doc frowned, the creases deepening in his forehead. "He claim you? He looks like he wants to kill me, but I'm not the enemy. My boyfriend is visiting his parents this weekend."

"No shit?" My eyes widened. "I'm happy for you," I said as I smacked his arm. "It's not you he's angry with. It's me," I tried to explain, but nothing made sense. "Cactus is mad at me because I ghosted him. Well—not him. His texts." I shook my head. "Nothing's going on."

"Is that right?" Doc raised an eyebrow. "He looks like he doesn't fuck around."

"What is he doing?" I asked. I didn't want to whip my head around, obviously searching for him.

Doc's hand tightened around mine, closing the distance between us. "You're not over whatever is going on, but you need to play this cool. Take a deep breath and pretend he's not walking this way."

"Go." I tried to step away from him, but he didn't release me. "I'm serious. I'll be okay, and you'll be safer on the opposite side of the room." We were friends, and I didn't want him directly in the eye of a pissed-off biker.

Doc looked over my head, eyes narrowing as if he was debating leaving.

"Please," I begged. "Go."

He tipped his head in Cactus's direction, slipping into the crowd.

"Asshole," I muttered. It wasn't Doc I was mad at.

"Who was that?"

"A friend." He wasn't touching me, but I could feel the heat from his body, and I imagined the flare of his nostrils as his breath danced over the skin between my neck and shoulder. "Promise me you'll leave him alone."

Cactus didn't respond as he wrapped his arm around my waist, holding me against him. He wouldn't ask questions as he removed threats.

"Promise me. He's just a friend."

His grip flexed around my waist, and I turned to face him. Cactus's face was blank, but fire burned behind his eyes. I could see the danger, the violence, underneath the surface. "Why him?"

We'd never held hands. Never kissed. I should have walked away, reminding myself why this could never happen. I tried to break his hold, but he only tightened his arm around me. "You want to be angry with me, fine. I'm not thrilled with you either. You don't get to hunt me down just to mark your territory. I'm nobody's property."

Cactus hummed, not saying a word, and it made me angrier. I wanted to push him into a fight, knowing I could let the words out and he wouldn't hold them against me. Yet, he remained silent.

"I don't understand you. You said you wouldn't have fought for me, so why are you now playing the jealous lover?"

He was about ready to respond when the music died. The lights came up, forcing most people to close their eyes at the sudden brightness. There were groans rising from the crowd, resembling the hangovers most of them would have tomorrow.

A fight had broken out at the bar, and just like that, the night had caught fire.

Chapter Nineteen

Bleeding Hearts

Roxy

"What the fuck were you thinking?" Scorpion yelled at Angelica, yanking her up from the barstool. The bar was full of patrons, but no one stepped in to help her as she stumbled.

"I was thinking with my dick. You're familiar with that," she shot back, regaining her balance.

I knew from experience that no one wanted to be on Scorpion's radar. He made snap decisions, not giving a fuck who he hurt. Yet, it didn't stop most of the women in the room from wanting a taste. Angelica was an exception. She stood toe-to-toe with him, not giving an inch. Rage surrounded them, tangible, as he screamed more insults directly into her face in the middle of the barn.

"Are you done?" she asked calmly. I thought Scorpion was going to hit her, and my feet shuffled a few steps forward. When I realized I was the only one moving towards the bar, I turned slightly, motioning for Cactus to do something. Angelica was his sister, and with how close they were, he should have been standing in front of her. Instead, his feet never left the dance floor.

"She can handle him." He held me by my elbow, but when I pushed against him to free myself, his grip tightened. "If I get involved, he'll swing faster," he whispered.

I made a face at him. "She's your sister," I pleaded.

"Trust me, he may back down now if I defend her, but that won't be the end. He will play emotional games, using Bri against her, until he thinks she's paid enough. There's no telling how long that will last, and he'll send me out of town as punishment."

A protector wouldn't stand by when he could deflect the situation. Cactus might have been right, but I hated standing next to him when all I craved was for him to do something. Anything. Somewhere underneath the logic was a man who was alright with letting his sister take the hits. *What did that mean for me?*

Scorpion didn't raise his voice. He didn't need to. No one dared to look away from him. "No wonder your daughter thought it was okay to whore it out in a cemetery." It wasn't surprising he knew, even though Cactus and Huck had taken care of it.

Angelica's hand came out, slapping Scorpion in the face. "You're right, I'm whoring it out, sitting at a bar fully clothed. You've slept with at least four club bunnies this week."

His face went pale, highlighting the red mark on his cheek. "You're the only one I'd ever let hit me. Don't do it again." He leaned forward, taking up her personal space.

She didn't bow down to him. Their lips were a breath apart. "They like to wait for me in the back parking lot to gloat. I'm done playing these games with you." Anyone watching this shitshow knew she wasn't in control.

"I shouldn't be getting a phone call saying you're in the bathroom fucking the bartender when you've always been mine."

Angelica shook her head. The bouncer had called Scorpion, lying about what she'd been up to. We'd checked on her repeatedly, and even if we didn't have rules in place, she'd never left that barstool. This was a ruse. She turned her back on him, but Angelica didn't get very far. Scorpion locked her arm in a tight grip.

"Stay here." He let her go, took two strides to the front of the bar and sucker-punched the bartender. I had to give the man credit. He held onto the bar, refusing to hit the ground. It didn't help him.

Still, no one interfered. The man threw a few weak punches, but when they didn't land, he went on the defensive. It was only slightly better. Scorpion delivered blow after blow, each one more vicious than the last, until the man's face was nothing more than a bloody pulp.

"Please," the man begged. "Fuck! Have a little mercy. I have kids."

Angelica flinched. I tried to join the fight, but Cactus held onto me. Lulu shifted in my direction, but she was too far from the scene to do anything, even if there had been something to do.

The bouncers moved through the crowd, finally coming to the bartender's aid. They'd been standing on the fringes, watching like everyone else. It would take more than a few of them to control Scorpion. He wasn't some drunk asshole. He was the president of the local one-percent motorcycle club. They would escort him out without warning until the next time this happened.

"Don't leave," Cactus told me. He moved with the rest of the club, each biker blocking a bouncer.

I caught Lulu's eye, nodding towards the front of the barn. It was time to go before they even realized we were gone. She nodded, making her way slowly towards me. We didn't need any bikers to suddenly understand we were leaving. They would just put guards on us, thwarting our escape.

Lulu and I made it to Angelica, and she let us guide her out of the place. None of us said a word as we got in the car. A fun girl's night had turned into a brawl, and we were so used to the violence, we didn't run.

We were almost to the motel when Angelica swiped at a tear. "Maybe I should see how much the saloon is worth and sell it."

"Where would you go, sweets?" Lulu whispered. She had known Angelica longer, but I thought Ang was too good at running the place. I couldn't see her ever giving it up.

"Anywhere but here."

"Now, you're talking nonsense." Lulu's voice broke into what seemed like a million pieces. "If you sell and take Bri, they'll win, and you'll always feel you're on the run."

I felt that. "It might be worse on the other side, but at least it's different. The only good thing? It wouldn't be this place."

Angelica turned in her seat. "You know from experience?"

"I've always picked the worst choice for me, but I've learned one thing since being here. You don't have to keep bleeding over old shit. Close it. Don't pick the scar. Otherwise, you'll be stuck in the same loop forever. Too bad we couldn't drown him in the pond."

"What about my brother? Is he a wound you're going to let scar before you leave?" A look passed between us. Her eyes were soft, as if she knew what I was already going to say, and a quiet agreement passed in the silence. She'd step aside, and once I was gone, pick up his pieces.

I didn't have the heart to tell her she was one reason I wouldn't stay for Cactus. "No. He's too busy taking care of everyone else first to remember how to relax. I won't force more on him."

We knew better, but we'd formed a friendship tied together with hope. Sometimes, hope's cruelest trick was pretending escape was real.

As I opened my motel door later, I looked over my shoulder. Hoping I'd hear a motorcycle turning into the parking lot. It was funny how I kept waiting for a sign to prove me right when I'd already walked away.

***

Cactus

Scorpion strutted towards his bike. "I'm going to the cage fight, if anyone wants to come with." I wouldn't care if the fucking thing blew up with him on it. He'd gotten his way in the bar, and now he was going to find a fight, like he hadn't had enough.

I said nothing, afraid something truthful would slip I wouldn't be able to take back. The last thing I wanted was all hell to break loose. If it did, I'd deal, but his attitude was getting old. I had one place I needed to be before she got any more wrong ideas.

She hadn't followed my instructions, dismissing them carelessly. I should have been angry. Fuck, I was furious. Underneath, there was something worse. For once in my adult life, I was afraid, and I hated the way it twisted through my heart.

If she had been in real danger, I would've lost my shit. This was a well-known bar. She hadn't been alone. This wasn't about her safety. It was about me.

She'd slipped away, and I wanted to yank her back to my side, but I couldn't. It would be the one thing that made her run faster, and I wouldn't have a fucking chance in hell of keeping her. I knew exactly where she was heading. Tonight had given her a better reason to ice me out. It wouldn't happen. I wouldn't let it.

"Which bitch are you running to?" Scorpion asked me.

I rubbed at my eyes, running my hand over my face before I answered. I needed a minute so I wouldn't jump off my bike and beat him to a bloody pulp. "What the fuck is wrong with you?"

"I protected what's mine, while you stood there like a pussy." He smirked, knowing he had me in a precarious position. "She'll never walk away from me, no matter how much you want her to."

If I had stepped in, there was no doubt in my mind, he would have made it worse for my sister, but Roxy saw it differently. She had wanted me to show strength. I didn't, and the disgust in her eyes wouldn't let me forget it.

"If you think I'm a bitch, challenge me." I leaned against the seat of my bike, crossing my legs at the ankles. I wanted to appear relaxed, when I was anything but. "She's not yours, and she's not standing around waiting for you either. You're just too stupid to realize you've lost her."

He stood from his bike, cracking his knuckles. "You think they'll follow you? I have never lost a fight. The rest of our territory fears the Saints because of me." Charging, he threw a punch the second he got close. I caught it and gave him one back, harder. My knuckles reddened as they grazed his cheek.

"Guys," Huck tried to step in, but Scorpion held his hand out, stopping him.

"You think you can take me? No fucking way." He swung at my side, but I stepped away just in time. Scorpion's fist caught the flaps of my club cut, but he left himself wide open. I slammed my fist into his gut, forcing a grunt from his lips. It didn't stop him. He tried to land a left punch, followed by an uppercut that nearly clipped my chin.

We hit the ground hard, and my weight landed on top of him. I kept swinging until my knuckles split. The blood mixed with the sweat. Scorpion dug his elbows into the sharp gravel, using the leverage to twist, bucking me off. He forced his fist into my gut. I couldn't catch my breath, but I wouldn't stop. Not now. I'd bowed down to him for far too long.

"Break it up." I thought that might have been Aces, but I didn't stop defending myself until a few brothers pulled Scorpion off of me. A few more grabbed me under my armpits, hauling my ass up to stand.

"What the fuck was that?" Definitely Tumbleweed. "We've never taken pot-shots at each other. You should have challenged him."

"You know, we've never had a wise man." Scorpion shook off the brothers holding him, swiping his bottom lip with his thumb. It hadn't split. "Maybe it's about time to retire our first one."

Is he really going for an age joke?

"Don't call me. I'll be busy at the cages." He swung his foot back over his bike, giving a fake salute before he roared out of the parking lot. He didn't need to look behind him, knowing most of the brothers would follow. Only the executives lingered near the bikes.

I eyed them, waiting for someone to take another swing. My fists clenched in anticipation. I came and went as I pleased, preferring not to bond over brotherhood. It didn't make me well-liked, but I did the job, and no one had ever had any complaints.

"I fucking told you this was fucking going to be bad." Tumbleweed spat his chew on the ground. He scanned me, looking for broken bones. I could have told him there were none. "I fucking called it, and no one listened to me."

"What the fuck are we supposed to do, huh?" Flash barked. "Scorpion scared the whole damn territory." He paced, shaking his head. "Now, I'm not the only one thinking his dick gets more action than his fucking brain." Flash's jaw clenched, turning to pace in the opposite direction. "Fear fades, and when it does? I don't want to go to war."

All of their heads turned in my direction. "I do my part for the club, and that's it. Don't look at me to lead the rebellion. I don't think any of us can fix him."

I swung my leg over my bike, heading towards the shitty motel. I knew where the damage had hit, but I had thirty minutes before I'd get my chance to stop the bleeding. One shot to make it right, or lose her for good.

Chapter Twenty

Come Hell Or High Water

Cactus

I parked my bike at the back of the saloon, preferring to walk to the motel. It bought me a few extra minutes before we squared off. I'd been waiting for this opportunity to fix things, but she'd ask questions I was afraid I didn't have the answers to.

You were only supposed to get her story.

She'd told me exactly who she was, but I had been so used to wading through the lies, I hadn't been paying attention.

It wasn't rocket science. I'd bet money no one had ever put Roxy first her whole life. She'd silently screamed at me every chance she got. She didn't know she was doing it. It wasn't a ploy. It was just who she was. Roxy liked to observe the world around her, finding pleasure in the small things. I should have been soaking up every detail, but I had only listened when it suited me.

If I were her, I would have walked away from me, too. She'd asked where her place was in my life, and I'd shut her down—no hesitation. She wouldn't fight to be heard. Her silence had said everything. She wasn't cutting me out, but she wouldn't beg for space. I wouldn't disappoint her again. If she asked to be let go, I'd have to release her.

Crossing the parking lot, I heard the gravel crunch under my boots. The air smelled like rain, but it was too early for monsoon season. The glowing cherry of a cigarette flared, catching my attention. There were a few men leaning over the second-story balcony.

Taking the stairs two at a time, I didn't slow until I reached the second-story landing. There were four men, including the one I recognized from the first time I'd tried to kick Roxy's door in. He'd thought it was just a fight with my Old Lady. I doubted he would give me any trouble, but they were too close to Roxy's room.

Knocking on her door wasn't part of the plan. She wouldn't answer if she knew it was me. I'd lost her respect. Picking her lock wasn't an option either—not with them watching. They'd see how easy it was. Getting her to talk to me was one thing, but I wouldn't put her in unnecessary danger.

My boots squeaked on the concrete, catching their attention.

"Hey man," the one I recognized said when he saw me at the top of the stairs. "You in trouble again?" He'd remembered. I didn't miss the irony. It hadn't been true then, but now was a different story. The other men laughed, assuming he was right.

"Did she ever give you a key?" he asked me. Turning back to his buddies, he pointed in my direction. "The last time I saw this guy, he was hitting the door with the heel of his boot, getting nowhere fast."

I shook my head, not saying a word. They didn't need to know my business, and I was running out of patience.

"I should be all neighborly-like." It only made the men in the group laugh harder. He took a step towards her door, his fist getting ready to knock. The scars on his knuckles shone in the moonlight. The contrast was a warning to anyone who wanted to step up. I wasn't a stranger to violence, but he looked like he'd fought to survive.

I wasn't interested in puffing my chest, proving I was the better man. This wasn't about him or his cronies, but I'd be damned if they thought they had a chance. I planted myself in front of her door, daring any of them to try me.

"You could ask for a cup of sugar." I didn't know which idiot had said it, but they slapped each other's backs, lighting up more cigarettes. The smoke curled around us in a haze.

They thought this was a joke. A lover's quarrel. I might have laughed with them years ago, but now I didn't see the point. This was about owning up to the damage I'd caused her. I wouldn't let them use her pain for entertainment, but if they kept this up, she'd shut all of us out.

"You won't be able to speak to her when I break your fucking jaws." The words rolled off my tongue, smoother than I expected. I had a few years on them, but I had earned my patch while they figured out how to shave. I grabbed the edges of my club cut, reminding them I was a Saint.

I'd only protected her when it was convenient for me, and I owed her one. She didn't need these assholes harassing her in this shitty motel.

Roxy must have heard the commotion because her door violently swung open, bouncing off the inside wall of her room. She appeared in the doorway, still dressed as she had been for the club—a sheer tank with spaghetti straps and a short skirt. There were slits on either side of her thighs, skin showing as she shifted her weight. Her hands clenched into fists. Her eyes glared, and I thought she might take a swing.

"Get the fuck out of my face," she told me through gritted teeth, shoving my side. I held my chuckle back as I shifted my stance, regaining my balance.

"Damn." There were a few wolf whistles. "Shit, I'd be a good boy if my woman looked like that."

She turned in their direction, freezing when she saw how close the four of them were. The other man still had his hand raised near the other side of the doorway. She paled but quickly regrouped. "Are you going to wrap up this pissing contest soon?"

I didn't let it show, but I was proud of her. I'd seen her freeze multiple times, and this was the first time she'd actually tried to fight back. It was progress. She didn't have to worry. I wouldn't let anything happen to her.

"If you want me to whip it out, we can measure the stream." The man lowered his arm, but he leaned into her space.

"Keep it in your pants, Romeo." She crossed her arms over her chest.

This was done. I turned toward her, putting my hands on her shoulders. "Come on, sweetheart." I thought I had been gentle as I tried to guide her backwards into the room. She shrugged me off, pushing me out the door. She tried to close it, but I quickly stuck my foot in the doorway, blocking her path.

"We're not doing this."

"Nope, we're not." She opened the door just enough to slam it again. I caught the edge, holding it before it hit my foot. If she locked the door, any chance to make amends would be over for me.

I'd had enough, and if we kept going like this, one of us was going to get hurt. I slung her over my shoulder, intending to set her on her feet inside the room, but she squirmed, fighting like hell. Her fists knocked against my back.

The door slammed behind us.

"I'm not doing this with you," she snapped, hitting her fist against my back. "Seriously, put me the fuck down. I'm not wearing underwear, asshole."

I said nothing, dropping her onto the bed. I'd heard the panty comment, but if I let my mind go there, I'd lose the only shot I had to fix this.

"When you're done fighting me, let me know." I grabbed the chair, dragging it to where she had no choice but to look at me.

"Call Aces and tell him to fix my car. I know he's waiting for your approval." She sat up, plopping the pillows behind her back, before crossing her arms and facing me. "I have the money."

"You don't have shit," I said, flinching at my own words. I'd been a biker too long. I'd never had to use words when fists were easier. That was where I kept fucking up with her.

It had slipped, but as I started to apologize, a plastic bag came flying at my head. My reflexes kicked in, catching it before the bag touched my nose. She'd been saving her tip money. At a glance, I could tell there was more than enough for her to leave.

"You're not going anywhere." I'd done it again. I couldn't make these mistakes with Roxy if I wanted her to believe in me. "I'm supposed to be owning my shit. You're right to break my balls at every turn," I said, dropping the bag onto the table next to me.

"Tell Aces to fix my car, so I can leave."

I slid further down in the chair. "You know that's fucking bullshit. This isn't about you leaving. This is about how I got caught with my guard down. You asked where you stood, and I froze. You're familiar with that."

"If you were so concerned, why didn't you call me back?"

"You gave me a chance to fix it, but the look on your face stopped me. You were done with my ass, and I hated I couldn't reassure you when you needed it." I rubbed a hand through my hair and down my face.

"I'm not your problem."

"No, but I make you my problem every time I can't walk away." I didn't stutter or look away from her. I wasn't sure where her head was after tonight, and I fully expected her to either throw a fit or ignore me.

I didn't expect her to laugh, the sound so brittle it struck a nerve in my chest.

"Do you even hear yourself right now? You're loaded down with responsibility. Your loyalty is to everyone else but yourself." She waved her hand in my direction. "You don't have room for one more, and I won't bleed for someone who can't take care of me."

"You think you have everything figured out?" I was listening, but if I didn't turn this conversation around, she'd think she was right. She was, if she only considered the past. I'd had plenty of time to think this through on the road.

"Obviously." Her tone was dry as she swung her legs over the bed. Sitting on the edge, she faced me directly, scrunching her nose. "I promised to stop the bleeding."

"What does that mean, stop the bleeding?"

"I was trying to be helpful in the car on the way back. I told Angelica to let the past scar. Stop picking it, and the bleeding will stop. I didn't realize I was talking to myself."

"Since I keep fucking up, you're going to leave. Stop the bleed, so that I don't hurt you?" I was unraveling, afraid she'd put the nail in the coffin of a relationship that hadn't even started.

"Something like that. I could destroy you, too."

She didn't raise her voice, and that sent a shiver down my spine. This scared me more than any time I'd ever seen my life flash before my eyes.

"I've gotten used to fixing everything. No one asks anymore." My leg bounced as I tried to plan a thought. "It wasn't what you asked, but the question itself. It threw me, and it's been fucking downhill ever since."

"Even if I forgave you, I don't know how I'm going to get past tonight. She's your sister, and you didn't move from my side. I was fine." She tucked a piece of hair behind her ear, a nervous tic, before getting up and pacing in front of the bed.

"Until Ang makes a final decision, they'll always play these games. She won't move on. Why? I don't know, and he won't let her go."

"The club comes first. Your family second." Roxy stopped, dropping her eyes to the ground. "You're exhausted from being everything to everyone. We're similar like that." She took a deep breath. "I won't be the final weight that breaks you."

"You should give me a chance to show you. These aren't empty words, sweetheart." I threw it out there, hoping she'd catch the pass. "Anytime you want to leave, tell Aces, and he'll fix your car."

"You're insane. Do I have a choice in any of this?" She stared down at me, scanning my face. Her eyes were sad, and I wasn't sure why. If I asked, wanting to fix whatever it was, I'd prove her point.

"Not really." I hated how fast I'd said that, but I wasn't ready to let her walk.

"That's what I thought. I didn't have a choice with the Disciples either, but I saved myself by running. I'm saying maybe, but you have to let me go if it breaks. If you break. I don't want to be chased."

It was easier to say nothing than make a promise I knew would be a lie. I would always fight for her, but there wasn't anything else for now. I stood up from the chair, tucking it under the small table near the door.

Pulling out my phone, I clicked some music channel, letting it stream into the room. She knew me only as Cactus—Sergeant at Arms. What she needed was Grant: the history buff, the traveler, and the man who had made choices based on other people's decisions. I slid my club cut off, hanging it from the back of the chair. It didn't belong in this moment.

"Dance with me," I said, standing in the gap between the bed and the outside window.

"Why?" The sadness disappeared as her brow furrowed, confused.

"You were busy when I got to the bar, and I didn't get a dance."

She sighed, slowing her steps before making her way over. "It's just a dance. Still not a yes, so leave him alone. He's just a friend."

I reached for her, taking her into my arms. "I waited too long after the video call."

"I deleted your texts without reading them."

"I know. Eights told me when he sent a picture of you in the saloon the morning after."

"I thought it was pretty self-explanatory." She tried to pull away, but I tightened my arms, making sure her cheek was against my shoulder.

"It was. I fucked up."

"I can't deal with fuck-ups. I'm too tired." She picked her head up, shifting back to look me in the eye. "I'm serious. I don't know who I am anymore. Everything's changing, and I don't want to drag you down with me."

The sadness was back in her eyes, and I understood. I couldn't blow smoke up her ass. She might have been young enough to be my kid, but she'd lived a life, and it had led her to the same mistrust I had.

"Let me bring you peace, the way you soothe my chaos." I slowly spun her as we swayed to the music. The song was something soft, but neither of us really heard it.

"I won't leave the club, but I'm not stuck here. You want to travel, I'll go back on the road as a nomad. You want to stay here, we stay here, but I need you to give me enough time to show you that this isn't all bullshit."

"Maybe." She laid her forehead against my sternum, wrapping her arms around my neck. "You make me want to feel," she mumbled.

Chapter Twenty-One

Doing The Historical Thing

Roxy

A week ago, I'd let a few walls crumble. I hadn't raised my voice, but I'd made sure he heard me, loud and clear. It was a first, and though I hated confrontation, I was proud every time I replayed it in my head.

Neither of us had given in. We were both convinced we were right. When Cactus left that night, I thought he'd fade into the background. I'd been wrong, thinking I wasn't worth the fight. It'd started again the next morning with a new text thread. Cactus never pushed beyond my limits, but I was a fool if I didn't think he was trying hard.

I'd underestimated how much thought he'd put into this. Cactus was a smart man, and while he didn't play emotional games, he gave me exactly what I needed. He'd order lunch from the saloon so he could visit for a few minutes. If he didn't make it into town, he still checked in. The little things made the difference, like when he walked me to and from the motel. We'd spend the trip swapping stories about our day, like normal people. He never stayed over thirty minutes, and it worked. Our silences said more than words ever could, but when he was gone, the quiet wasn't comforting. It was hollow.

Cactus had shown up during the re-enactors' visit this week, waiting for his lunch. He'd seen the lunch crowd and had stood in the corner with his back against the wall. I hadn't seen him walk in, too busy keeping the kids moving, but I hadn't been able to shake the feeling someone was watching me. This time, he had winked as he walked out the door. I wasn't invisible in a room of parents and tourists, but the person I had wanted to notice had. My smile was brighter and wider the rest of the day.

Doc wasn't the only one who noticed. The girls had tried to get the details out of me, but all I had said was, "Everything's good." They'd pushed, but I'd held firm. I wouldn't listen to their biased opinions. For two emotionally stunted people, we were crawling. It was good for now.

Lying in my bed, I stared straight up at the popcorn ceiling. There were blobs I didn't stop to analyze too closely. It was Saturday, and while I would have preferred to be working, Lulu and I always let the high school girls get extra hours. Today, I didn't mind. I needed a break from prying eyes continually poking where their noses shouldn't be.

I picked up my head, searching the ledge where I kept my groceries. I hoped that if I stared at it long enough, the coffee would brew by itself. It was a dream. Microwaving a pack of instant coffee wasn't appealing. Staying in bed and turning the TV on seemed like the best plan.

I was flipping through the channels when there was a heavy knock on my door. Cactus normally picked my lock, so if this was one of his new tactics, he'd let himself in. I ignored it.

No one needed to know I was a woman staying by myself. They could suspect, but I'd never advertised my status. I constantly saw the four men who'd been hanging out on the balcony. They'd say hello when they saw me, asking how my man was. I lied and told them he was amazing and thanked them for asking.

Another heavy knock beat on the outside of my motel door. I still ignored it, but when I heard scratching against the lock, the corners of my lips turned. Those sounds could mean only one thing. Lying on my side, I pulled the blanket up to my chin, settling in to wait.

The door popped open, and there he was, blocking out the outside light. His eyes found mine, a smirk settling on his lips. "Get dressed," he said, standing in the doorway.

"What happened to 'Hi, how are you?'" I shuffled deeper under the covers.

He stepped into the room, letting the door slam shut behind him. "How come you don't have the chair underneath the handle?" Cactus pulled it out from underneath the small desk, taking a seat to prove his point.

"Baseball cap? No club cut? What's wrong with you?" If I hadn't known better, I would have thought he was a regular guy, out for the day. It wasn't hard to see how handsome Cactus was for an older man. I allowed myself one quick look, and then I shut those thoughts down.

"You didn't answer me."

"Why would I jeopardize my safety by telling a biker?" If he wanted to break down the door, the chair wouldn't stop him.

He raised his eyebrow at me, shifting his ass so that his legs spread open.

"I thought about getting a decent coffee this morning, but then I'd have to get up and thought better of it. You?" I pulled the covers under my chin.

He wrinkled his nose, ignoring my question. "You've got two choices. One: get dressed, and we'll grab decent coffee on the way. Two: I drag you, kicking and screaming, and whatever you've got on is it. Go with option two."

"You'd like that way too much." I rolled my eyes, knowing I had a T-shirt and a pair of pajama shorts on. It wasn't like he was going to get skin. He stood up from the chair and made his way over to my suitcase. "Don't touch my underwear. We've gone over this."

"What underwear? There are barely any clean clothes in here." He shuffled my stuff around. I could have told him it was a waste of time. "Why don't you come stay with me? This place isn't really that safe for you, and we have a washer and dryer. I'll even buy the fancy detergent."

I searched his face, looking for the punchline, but all I saw was worry in his brown eyes. His mustache ticked, as if he was giving me time to think this over, but he'd already decided what was best. "Fuck, no. You live in the clubhouse."

"My room is larger than this one." He looked around before staring at me down the bridge of his nose. "It's also cleaner."

"Your room might be, but I'm having visions of a frat house crossed with a sex dungeon. No, thanks. I'll stay here."

He said nothing, and I must have been closer to the truth than I realized.

Cactus dropped a pair of shorts and a T-shirt onto my leg. "Get dressed. Please, sweetheart."

I sighed, sinking into the mattress. It was the please that softened me. "What's so important?" I asked him.

"You're off. I'm off...today. Figured you would want to do the historical thing." Cactus shrugged, and it made him look younger for a second.

I threw the covers off. The clothes fell to the floor as I stood on top of the bed. "I've never done the historical thing," I said excitedly. This was going to be a fun day, nothing more.

"You won't be now if you crack your head open. Come here." He held out his arms to me, and I let him lift me from the bed until my feet touched the floor. Neither of us moved, but we held onto each other a beat. "Go. Time's ticking." He reached down and swatted my ass.

I shook my head and smiled. I was ready in under ten minutes.

***

We made small talk, heading towards the main street, but before we turned the corner, he stopped. "Don't laugh," he said.

My laughter was already bubbling to the surface, but it died when I noticed how hesitant he was. His fingers flexed as if he wanted to bolt, but something held him in place. I went to grab his arm for comfort, unsure how else to help. He wouldn't look directly at me.

"The only original building on the main drag is the theatre," he rushed. "The tourism volunteers will add the saloon to that, but I'm not sure if that's actually true. Mixed accounts." His shoulders hunched as if he were afraid of revealing a secret.

I didn't understand what was happening, but I wouldn't leave him. This date... *Could I even call it one?* His face was blank, but his eyes danced back and forth, staring straight ahead. "You don't have to shrink to talk about something you love," I whispered. "There's nothing wrong with liking pieces of history." I reached for his hand, locking our fingers together. "Come on, tour guide, you promised me a historical day and a good cup of coffee."

His lips tipped up at the corners, moving with me. We turned the corner, but when we reached the Blue Angel, he bypassed it. Continuing up the street, Cactus turned into a small bakery that was squeezed between two trinket shops. "Don't tell my sister or Lulu, but they make better coffee here," he said as he held the door open for me.

"Your secret is safe with me." I squeezed his hand in solidarity.

We ordered, and when the little old lady with her pink apron handed us our cups, she said we looked like a cute couple and hoped we had fun today. She moved towards the back of the coffee shop as we took a seat at a table.

He let his guard slip for a minute. I'd never been greedy, knowing what it was like to go without, but I wanted as many pieces as I could get of him for myself. Cactus, the biker, was as safe for me as Grant, the man. I doubted he knew his niece had revealed that part of him. "How did you get here?"

This was the first relationship I'd ever had where I cared to look beyond the surface. Caring hadn't been part of the plan. Staying, even less so, but here I was, digging for the emotional parts of him no one had touched.

"My mother used to bring us here when we were kids for day trips. It holds a lot of good memories for me, so when I didn't have a plan, I found myself here." Before he said anything else, his phone rang. Pulling it out, he checked the screen before answering. "What?" He listened, making a face at me over whatever the person on the other line was saying. "I'm not on club business, so I don't need a babysitter." He swallowed the rest of the coffee before returning to the conversation. "Get off my dick."

There's the prick. I smiled behind my cup as I finished my coffee.

"Don't even think about it." Cactus ended the call before turning his phone off. "The brothers are bored, and their favorite pastime is to be as fucking annoying as possible," he said to me.

I smiled, tossing my cup. He held the door for me, but as soon as I stepped onto the walkway, I heard the cowboys up the street starting their routine.

"Do you want to stay and watch them?" Cactus bent down and whispered in my ear.

"I've seen this part a few times," I teased, standing close to the railing so that I could see the show.

"I'm sorry I missed the first time you played along." His breath tickled my ear, sending a shiver down my spine.

"Lulu asked me if I wanted to bag a Clanton or an Earp. I think I prefer a cactus. Besides, she told me we'd make money. That's all I cared about then." I leaned back against him, and his arm instantly wrapped around my middle. It felt possessive, and I let it feed into my fantasy of being appreciated.

Coming to Tombstone had just been about a paycheck and a busted car. I never expected to find something real after I'd run from something awful. This wasn't all sunshine and roses. It was terrifying in a way I'd never experienced. This man was dangerous, and I honestly believed what I'd said to him. We each had the power to destroy the other, and I'd never see the gaping hole in my chest until I was already gone.

I wasn't someone who usually showed emotion over simple things, but the excitement sizzled in the air, making it impossible to stay numb. I smiled, wanting to absorb as much of it as possible. It reminded me of when the world had held answers instead of warnings. The re-enactor playing Ike Clanton for the day lumbered down the street in front of us.

"My head," he moaned, stumbling around, before taking a fake sip from the bottle he used as a prop. I thought I would just be another tourist in the crowd, but he recognized me. Tipping the bottle in my direction, Ike wagged his finger at me. "You're trouble. Brought here by the devil." He tripped, stumbling over his feet a few times. He positioned himself close to the rail. "Ms. Roxy."

Cactus's arm tightened around my waist, eliminating any space between us. "Don't get attached to his character. Ike showed up at the O.K. Corral unarmed. You don't want someone like that." He made a humming sound. "I've never backed down from a fight."

The corner of my lip turned up. I didn't pay him any attention, knowing if I did, it would just encourage this Neanderthal behavior. Secretly, I didn't mind. I'd been around enough motorcycle clubs to know how possessive they could be. This was Cactus staking his claim in a way that didn't scare me. The snippets of history were nerdy but cute.

I bent backwards, thinking I'd get his attention. It didn't work, so I slid my fingers between his at my waist, squeezing. "If I forget to thank you for today, thank you. I'm having a good time." I meant every word, but it had also been a ploy to distract him.

There was a family standing next to us at the rail, but the grandmother had her mouth open. "I know you from somewhere."

"No," I laughed, not wanting her to draw attention to me. She'd probably seen the video and couldn't put two-and-two together without my saloon girl uniform. "I work at the Blue Angel," I said, heat rising to my cheeks in embarrassment. I didn't want her persistence to ruin the day with Cactus by bringing up bad memories.

The cowboys were loud enough that we could still hear them up the street.

"I know I saw one of the Clantons running down here."

They appeared, and I wanted to jump up and down like the little kid next to me. These four were the men who always ate lunch at the saloon. I wasn't sure it would have been as fun if it were another set of actors the city employed.

"I'm telling you, Wyatt. He was here. Can't you smell the wasted liquor?" Doc hit the marshal in the arm, pretending to sniff the air. "One should never take good liquor in vain."

"If he's drunk, he can sober up in a jail cell."

"You know he is, but I want to know if he's stupid enough to bring his gun into town." Morgan Earp flapped the edges of his duster coat as he strolled down the street. "The Clantons are a stain on society. Speaking of stains, I haven't seen a red sash."

"No one likes a snitch," Doc drawled.

A chuckle spread through the crowd on both sides of the street.

"Well...I'm ready for lunch, so if we don't find him, you all know where to find me," the man playing Virgil Earp said.

Had Angelica made a deal with the city? That was weird. She'd talked about making the cowboy visits permanent, but I had heard nothing concrete.

"Not me. If Clanton doesn't show, I'm going to bed." Doc Holliday stood at the end of the street, twirling his cane. He stabbed the end into the dirt, leaning against it as he struck a pose, yawning.

"You probably spent all night playing poker," Morgan laughed.

"You would know, ole boy. You were sitting next to me."

Another laugh spread through the crowd.

"Besides," Doc said, "my favorite saloon girl is off, so there's no point in going." He tipped his hat in my direction, sending the grandmother next to me spiraling again.

I squeezed Cactus's hand.

"You're my favorite saloon girl, too," he whispered directly into my ear, sending a shiver down my spine.

Doc started to say something else, but there was a loud boom. The cowboys took off running towards a side door. They disappeared, and a volunteer from the O.K. Corral came out of their shop, offering tickets to the show.

"Do you want to go?" I turned to ask Cactus.

He pulled two tickets from his pocket, swishing them between his fingers.

"What if I had said no?" I smiled. There was no way he hadn't planned all of this, and my heart gave an extra beat before my chest warmed from within. He reached for my hand, guiding me towards the entrance.

"Come on, sweetheart. Wouldn't want to disappoint your fans." He was kidding, but there was just enough bite in his tone that I could barely tell the difference. I didn't want to be with anyone else, but if I told him that, I'd be the one scaring him. A knot settled in my chest, excitement racing towards panic. He must have felt it, holding my hand.

His fingers curled around mine, steady and sure. I hated how much I needed that. Needed him. "Turtles," he said. "They crawl at their own pace, like us." The knot in my chest loosened.

Chapter Twenty-Two

The Phoenix Rises

Cactus

I'd spent all morning preparing for a three-day run with Tumbleweed. Drug shipments were coming across the border, and they'd paid us for protection. I'd signed up for this the moment I'd accepted the patch, but Roxy hadn't. I wasn't leaving without seeing her first. Picking her up from the motel, I'd taken her to a local restaurant for dinner.

We were riding out first thing in the morning, which left little time. I needed to tell Roxy what to expect. Besides, I enjoyed spending time with her, banking the memories for when the quiet got too heavy.

She sat across from me, snickering each time the vinyl creaked when she shifted. Her eyes were bright, but she barely held back the yawns. The exhaustion was hard to ignore as it crept in.

I leaned back, buying a few seconds to find the right words. "I'm scheduled for a run this weekend." She'd be fine. I just needed to be straight with her.

"Okay." She took a deep breath. "When are you coming back?" she asked, wiping her lips with a napkin.

"Three days, hopefully." I shrugged. "I won't be available, and I didn't want you to think you were alone. If you need something, you call Angelica."

"She's my boss. I'm not calling her on a weekend. I appreciate the thought, but I'll be fine by myself."

If I hadn't been watching her so closely, I would have missed the mischief settling in her eyes. Placing her elbows on the table, she batted her eyelashes at me. "Maybe I'll hook up with a cowboy." She smirked, teasing.

"Sure. Most of them live with their mothers—basements and all." I folded my arms against my chest as I watched her.

She mirrored my position, a grin tugging at the corner of her lips. "I could definitely do younger, but not sure about hotter." We stared at each other until she broke first, laughing as she reached for her glass. "I won't do that. Be safe, and I'll be here when you get back."

When I dropped her back off at the motel, I held her longer than usual. I thought about leaving, but she buried her face in my neck, and I wasn't ready to let go. Neither of us spoke. We didn't need to.

This was the slowest I'd ever taken things with a woman, but it felt right with her. After she'd held my hand, I'd tested the boundaries, experimenting to see how far she would allow me to go. I could throw an arm around her, and she wouldn't flinch, but hugging was new. In a few weeks, I might get a kiss. For now, this was enough.

"You take care of yourself," she mumbled against me. "Be selfish." Her words hit harder than I expected.

I wasn't sure how long we stood there, but Roxy pulled away first. She kissed my cheek, saying goodnight before sprinting up the steps to her room. I waited, watching to make sure she got in all right before I took off.

She opened her door and flipped on the light. I thought she'd head inside, but she paused, turning around. Waving to me from the balcony, she stood there an extra second.

Hopefully, three days would go by quickly. After that, I'd take her somewhere nice. Maybe then, she'd finally kiss me.

Maybe not.

Crawling.

***

The glow from the red light bathed my bike as I sat, engine idling. I scanned my surroundings, tension simmering under my skin. My leg bounced as I drummed against my thigh. No one else was on the road. Unusual even for a small town like Tombstone. Something was off. The stillness was eerie.

A high-pitched squeal ripped through the silence. Crotch rockets streaked into view. Their headlights flared in my mirrors, blinding me. The light turned green. I wasn't fucking around. I took off.

I cruised through a few more green lights before the next one turned red on the outskirts of town. I glanced in my mirror—two bikes, barely a few lengths behind my back tire. If they were trying to be inconspicuous, they fucking sucked at it.

Turning right, I pretended I hadn't seen them. I made another sharp cut, easing off the gas to bait them. They swerved, barely taking the curve as their bikes hugged the ground. Predators—and I was the prey. There was no chance of calling in reinforcements.

The clubhouse was out. They'd kill me on the deserted road. No saloon. No motel. It was night, and there wouldn't be enough people around. Police station? Fuck, no. *Keep moving.*

No doubt now. This was a tail. The sport bikes screamed every time they hit the throttle. I'd started blowing through yellow lights, lucky that Tombstone was a small town with little traffic. Stopping wasn't an option. Not if I wanted to keep breathing.

I could see the bikers in my side mirrors. Full-face, black helmets. No patches. No identifiers. Bulletproof vests tight against their chests. Ghosts on bikes.

A crack tore through the air. Not a firework. The biker on the left fired at my tires. I ducked, zigzagging in the middle of the street as more shots rang out. *I won't make it past forty.*

I'd stopped looking for death to find me. It was inevitable, but this was a fucking shitty way to go. Shot in the back. During a gunfight. In Tombstone. It was a coward's way to die, but at least I wouldn't be the only one going down.

I sent up apologies to Roxy and my family, in case there really was some higher power. I'd done what I could for them, leaving them enough money that they would never go without. It was the least I could do.

I had just accepted my fate when the two bikers made a U-turn, speeding off in the opposite direction.

Was that supposed to be a scare tactic? Were they after me, *or had they seen my patch*? It didn't matter. Message received. Loud and clear.

My stomach churned, fighting the urge to puke as I mounted the clubhouse's front stairs, still processing what had happened on the road. The adrenaline still coursed through me, the line between rage and passion blurring with each step. I could hear the moans as soon as I opened the front door.

There'd been a time when I would have walked straight into the main room, picked whichever girl I wanted and fucked her until I had my fill, especially after dodging death. Now, there was only one woman who could light a fuse in me, and I wouldn't fuck it up for some cheap, meaningless thrills.

Leaning against the inside of the main door, I counted on the noises ending soon. I'd rally the troops, preparing for the battle that lay ahead. We hadn't had a club meeting in months, and I had a better chance of corralling the brothers if they were in between rounds. They needed to know what we were up against.

High-pitched shrieks stabbed at my skull, each one pulsing behind my eyes. Sweat thickened the air, the stench so bad it would take days to forget. Every piece of furniture had a woman bent over it, an offering nobody had to earn. No one was going to clean up the mess. The brothers would bitch, finding questionable fluids. I used to lose myself in shit like this until there was nothing left but silence. Tonight was different.

The patch always drew women in. It didn't matter what they looked like. There was always more, but we'd chased pussy over club protection. While I'd been swerving, dodging bullets, the brothers were ball-deep in distraction.

Aces had two women tied to the pool table. He rolled a billiard ball between their thighs, letting the smooth surface glide across their skin. They begged him for more, but he was busy giving the redhead between Eights' legs pointers. "Dude's not even moaning. You know how he likes it. Use your teeth." The executive team was following its leader.

I scanned the room, looking for Scorpion. My president was busy with his own set of blondes. He was sitting in his corner of the couch, letting Blonde A bounce in his lap.

"I'm next," Blonde B said, sitting next to him and rubbing her breasts in his face. "Come on, baby." She shoved his hand between her legs as she rubbed her nipple against his lips. "I know what you like," she moaned. It was all fake, but he didn't call her out on it.

"Hey," I said, my voice tight as I dropped onto the arm of the chair next to them. I'd prospected for loyalty. Brotherhood. Not this. We'd sold it all for pussy. "We need a club meeting tonight. Now."

"I'm busy." He continued to bite the blonde's tits. She'd wear bruises in the morning like a badge of honor.

I wouldn't talk club business in a room full of club bunnies. There could be spies, and it wasn't worth the risk. "Put your dick away for a second and be the president." I wasn't spelling it out for him. I'd seen the signs. The bikes. The clothing. It wasn't a coincidence. "The wrist tattoos. The phoenix has risen."

He pulled away from the blonde sitting next to him. "Don't stop," he said to the one riding his dick. "If you do, I'll kick you out, and you'll have to deal with the in-town dick."

My gut twisted as he pointed to the corner, crooking his finger. He was calling someone over. I followed his line of sight, and my chest clenched. This had nothing to do with her, but she'd become Scorpion's punchline. Eights had saved us the first time, letting me know to enter the clubhouse from the back. She wouldn't get lucky twice. There was nowhere for me to run.

She strutted across the room, her high heels clicking against the wood floor. A skirt too tight. She dressed like the other women, but something about her seemed too good for this. A year ago—hell, six months ago—I would have flipped up her skirt, bending her over the arm of the couch without a second thought. Now, I wasn't even hard. I'd outgrown casual sex.

"Don't make her the butt of your joke. I'm not interested." This was going to end badly for her. He wouldn't listen, continually feeding her lies to keep her chasing. Scorpion wasn't trying to win her. He was trying to get under my skin, so he'd have a reason to get rid of me.

"You need to get laid," he said to me, smirking. "Delilah actually gives decent head." The room laughed. This was exactly what I'd been trying to avoid.

"No," I barked, but she tried to straddle my lap anyway. I stood, the shift in my legs bucking her off of me. She landed on the floor with a loud thump. Laughter cracked around the room, louder this time. She didn't move, her arms crossed over her legs, as her eyes glistened. She never lowered her gaze, trying to let the room know this wasn't affecting her as badly as they wanted it to.

"You alright?" I asked her, holding my hand out to help her up. The entire room had gone silent, watching this exchange. This wasn't about Delilah. It wasn't about when Scorpion had tried to use her as a larger substitute for Roxy, or any of those other asinine things. This was about Scorpion reminding me of my place in the club.

She said nothing, eyes locked on mine. Delilah was another pawn in one of his games.

"He knows I'm not interested. He's using you to fuck with me." I left her where she was, heading towards my room.

"I'm thinking about having lunch at the saloon while you're gone. My dick might be diseased, but so is yours, considering where you've been." He was talking about the girls at El Sombra Roja's warehouse. Roxy had just arrived, but I hadn't accepted the cartel's gift. No one knew that, but he'd do anything to fuck with her mind. She was another person who would unwillingly play his games.

"I've never gone against you as my president. I've always been a good soldier, but if you lie to Roxy, I'll take your Butterfly away from you. You won't be able to find them." I turned to face the room. "That goes for all of you. Don't fuck with mine." I strolled to my room, not giving them any sign of how much I was fucking fuming.

Chapter Twenty-Three

The Slowest Burn

"When's the company-sponsored spa day?" Lulu asked Angelica just as a breeze drifted in through the kitchen door. The girls had wondered if customers would show now that the temperatures were bearable. Today's line stretched out the front door and around the corner, three shops down. As soon as one table cleared, Angelica seated the next family. One after another, until my corset clung to my skin, drenched in sweat. No one wanted to ask how long we'd be able to keep up this pace.

"Don't get me wrong, but your girl is tired." Lulu walked out the door, turning around to face us when she stepped into the parking lot. "Spa day." She gestured wildly, like a game show hostess revealing the grand prize.

Lulu was right. Days had become weeks, each running into the next. It was mid-September, and in the two months I'd been here, I'd started calling Tombstone home.

Angelica yawned. "I've thought about it, but nothing works. The dining room isn't big enough to bring in another waitress. The sections would be too small." She examined her fingernails, picking at a cuticle. "We could go to Tucson for the day."

"Is that a yes?" Lulu grabbed Angelica by her shoulders. "Don't tease me like this."

Angelica laughed, gently shrugging Lulu off. "It's a maybe."

"That's mom code for no," I teased. A motorcycle rumbled down the street, and we all watched, waiting to see who the biker was.

Lulu flicked her ponytail off of her shoulder. "I'm not the only one looking worse for wear. We could escape for an entire weekend. Pampering. Sleeping. Pure heaven."

Cactus pulled into the lot, parking his bike right in front of where we stood. We hadn't made plans for tonight, so this was a surprise. "Ladies," he said, removing his helmet, a faint smile tugging at the corner of his lips.

"Help me convince your sister to do a spa weekend." Lulu framed Angelica's face with her hands. "She needs to be rejuvenated, and you wouldn't deny your favorite sister and her best employees a treat, would you?"

"She's my only sister." He laughed, a low, gruff sound as his eyes lit up. I scanned him instinctively. In the beginning, I'd constantly waited for him to snap—collapsing under the weight of it all. Cactus was learning how to relax, and with every softened look on his face, my fears eased a little more. He wouldn't leave me prematurely.

"Ang needs to move on." He winced. Scorpion had been coming to the saloon more often. While I wasn't afraid he'd physically hurt me, I hated the psychological games he played with Angelica. He'd show up either right before the cowboys or right after.

Most days, Angelica ignored him. Every so often, he'd catch her unguarded, long enough for pretty words and empty promises. He'd be around more to make a go at something real. If she turned him down, he'd follow it up with what her heart wanted the most. He wanted to be a better father. His side chicks would then show up as she was leaving, shattering the illusion. She was lonely in a crowd, reaching for the version of herself he had always taught her to question.

"Pick a place, and I'll pay for the trip." His face went blank, but the twitch underneath his eye gave him away. Cactus didn't care if we went on a weekend trip. He cared about our safety.

"Yes!" Lulu pumped her fists in the air, twirling in the parking lot of the saloon. She dragged me with her, laughter bubbling up before I could stop it.

Angelica laughed heartily, walking over to Cactus. She wrapped one arm around his neck for an awkward side hug. "You don't have to do this. Thanks."

"Me too!" Lulu danced some more, gyrating to the music that played in her head.

"You need to find someone worthy of you." He cleared his throat. "I won't say a word if you suddenly start dating, as long as they're decent."

"We'll see." Angelica squeezed his shoulder before pulling away.

"More mom speak for now," I chimed in, and she shot me a look.

"See if you get any more $50 tips."

"Hey, I earned that. They were weird, and I nearly had a heart attack when I thought they'd walked out on the check." The warmth drained from Cactus's face. His jaw tensed, gaze sharpened, always scanning for danger. He'd circle back, pressing me to walk him through every detail.

"When are you making lasagna?" he asked Angelica, shifting her attention away from me.

"Whenever you want, as long as you bring Roxy." She kissed his temple before pulling away. "I know," she sighed. "I'm not ready to let go."

She said goodnight and walked off as Lulu chased her to her car, her voice animated as she tried to sell the idea of a spa day. "You can't say no to Cactus paying."

My feet moved on their own as the quiet settled around us. I rarely went in for public displays of affection, but I stepped into him, anyway. My arms wrapped around his neck without a second thought. He slid one of his arms around my back, and everything in me settled into place. I breathed him in, smelling of sunshine and leather. He'd been out riding all day.

"Hi," I whispered, placing my forehead against his.

His arm tightened around me, and I swore I felt him draw me in with each breath. I pretended I didn't notice for fear I reeked of saloon food and sweat.

"Come on," he murmured. "I brought dinner. Thought we'd watch the sunset from the overlook."

***

"That was delicious, thank you." I put my trash back in the bag before sticking my legs out in front of me. Cactus would never let me on his bike wearing my uniform. He'd thought of everything, bringing me a pair of my jeans and a sweatshirt.

"It's hot deli from the grocery store. Nothing special." I wouldn't argue with him over food, but it was better than anything I would have had tonight. The microwave had officially died, and I was living on delivery. There was only so much saloon food I could eat after serving all day.

Quiet settled around us, and I thought about testing a new limit. I wanted to feel the softness of his lips against mine. We'd come close several times before but had never crossed that line. I didn't think he'd say no, but kissing was more intimate than touch. He'd never made me feel uncomfortable, and if he turned me down, I'd respect that.

Tapping his leg, I waited, but he studied me out of the corner of his eye. I sat up on my knees and faced him, tapping his leg again. He needed to follow my lead without my asking.

His legs shifted, creating enough space for me to sit between them. I reached out to smooth the lines of his forehead. I traced the bridge of his nose, over to his cheek—the skin weathered from years of riding. His mustache twitched as I followed it from the top of his lip to the end, where it curled slightly. Using my other hand, I trailed the same path on the other side.

This was it. The intensity of his gaze held me captive. I'd never had someone see me so clearly, and it was overwhelming. I leaned forward, touching my lips to his before quickly pulling back.

"Kiss me," he exhaled.

I placed my hands on his shoulders, leaning in. This time, I licked his lips, begging for something, anything. He granted me entry, parting his lips to connect with mine. I wanted to remember every detail, no matter how small.

Everything was blurry in the heat of his kiss. I grabbed fistfuls of his T-shirt, anchoring myself to him so that I wouldn't float away. I had been the one to start this, but he kissed me like he needed it. Deep, slow, and then demanding. When I gave in, his control slipped, only making me want him more. It should have scared me, knowing my dating history, but Cactus would never hurt me, and I believed that with every fiber of my being.

"Grant," I breathed into the space between us. He buried his hands in my hair, lightly tugging at the roots.

"Say it again." His voice was hoarse.

I kissed him, lips pecking until we found the right combination. He'd attack until I whimpered against his mouth, pulling back until I reignited our heat. "Grant." When I couldn't breathe, I laid my head against his shoulder as he held me.

He shifted me in his lap until his chest pressed against my back. His arms wrapped around me tight as he placed a kiss on my temple. "Tell me about today." His voice rumbled in my ear.

"There were four of them," I started, watching as the sun set in bright orange. "They walked in with their helmets still on, but that wasn't the weird thing. They ordered the same meal, cooked the same way, and when I brought the food, they all ate with the same hand." I shifted, trying to get closer to his body. "This was the worst part. They all had the same tattoo on the inside of their wrists."

"You said you thought they stiffed you," he prompted.

"Yeah, I went to run another table's food, and when I turned around, they were gone. I thought I was going to owe Angelica, but on the table was $150. I kept the $50, and the rest paid for their bill."

"How did they look?"

"Black clothing, but I'm sure they wore contacts and dyed their hair the same shade. They even held their helmets while they ate." His body tensed as I talked. "Is something wrong?"

"Not sure, but if they come back, call me." He placed a kiss on my neck, sliding his tongue up to my ear. "I'll fight for you."

I thought about reigniting the fire from our kisses, but a raindrop hit the back of my hand. *Does it really rain in Arizona?* A few more scattered across the sleeve of my sweatshirt, leaving dark spots behind. The rain felt like the promise of something brand new.

"Yes," he chuckled, answering me. I must have asked out loud. "It does, but we need to go. There's only one road on this mountain, and if it rains, we could be stuck in a flash flood."

He turned onto the main road as the rain poured. It felt like a clean slate, washing away the part of me that used to hurt. I no longer needed to brace for disappointment.

Chapter Twenty-Four

Let The Rain Fall

Roxy

We rushed through the motel room door, soaked through after riding the entire way back from the overlook. There hadn't been a single overpass to shelter under. I ran straight for the bathroom, gathering as many towels as I could find.

"Here." I threw one at Cactus. He'd already taken off his club cut, letting it hang off the back of the chair, but his gray shirt clung to his skin. It highlighted the tattoos in bright colors. If they had been shades of gray, I would have understood, but the color had been the fun he'd been suppressing for a long time.

He peeled his sodden T-shirt off, flinging drops across the room before it landed on the floor. The faint clink of his belt snapped me out of it. I startled, not realizing I'd been staring.

His jeans hit the floor next to his shirt, the muscles in his thighs flexing as he shifted his weight. Quickly, I stripped off the sweatshirt and jeans, revealing my uniform underneath. I hadn't wanted to waste time earlier, preferring to pull the jeans over the shorts in the parking lot. They were tight enough I had had no trouble smoothing the fabric out underneath the denim.

There was no finesse, no slow striptease. My uniform was stuck to me, and although I was wearing a bra and panties underneath, I didn't take it off. Every layer was a shield, the only thing between me and heartbreak.

"Come here." He crooked his finger at me, holding a towel. I didn't move, and my mouth went dry. "Sweetheart? You okay?"

A quiet sob escaped before I could stop it. It was raw, unfamiliar, tangled in longing I didn't understand. I froze, not from fear but yearning. Cactus stood in his boxers, rainwater dripping, and I wanted to be so close to him to quiet the ache.

"Hey." He was standing in front of me, but all I could see was his chest. Cactus's fingers brushed my cheek, then tipped my chin gently until I met his eyes.

"It's not fear," I said, trying to explain. "It's..." I didn't have the words. He was a man, and I'd only been with boys. This was the weight of wanting to be enough for him. To provide everything he needed, like he already had for me.

"I get it," he said, bringing the towel up and scrunching the ends of my hair. "If you say no, nothing is going to happen." He dragged the towel down my neck and over my chest. "I'm a man, and I can control my urges."

He kissed my collarbone, lingering for a moment, before moving to dry off my arm. He did the same thing on the other side. I let out another breath-like sound before throwing myself in his arms. I couldn't remember the last time I had cried, but my tears mixed with the rain, running down my cheeks.

"Who hurt you?" he whispered into the stillness of the room, holding me tightly.

"No one. Just a lot of close calls." I dug my nails into his back, trying to transfer my pain. Cactus was strong enough to bear my sins. "I...I've never been with someone who didn't use sex as a weapon." My forehead rubbed against his sternum. "This isn't fear." My lips pressed against his skin. "This is all the times I was told I wasn't good enough. It's irrational, but you're the hottest man I've ever seen."

The muscles in his arms twitched as he chuckled. My forehead bounced with the vibrations from the sound. "Trust me. You say no, I dry you off, and we watch TV in bed." He tipped my chin up again to gaze into my eyes. "Change your mind? Say the word, and the outcome will be the same. TV in bed."

It was the promise I needed to hear. "I'm not sure. I want to...but—"

"TV it is," he murmured. He didn't sound frustrated. It was more of an acceptance, and that hurt more than anger ever could. "Don't worry. When it's right, I'll be the one who can't get enough of you."

I tried to laugh, but another sob escaped.

"Let me help you with this. You might feel better dry."

I nodded, though my fingers curled tighter against his back, not ready to let go. He unhooked the bottom of the corset, working his way up. Cactus picked up a dry towel, dragging it across my shoulders, down to the soft dip between my breasts, and across my stomach, hips, and thighs. He treated me as something fragile. Beautiful but breakable.

Leading me by my hand, he made sure I was comfortable, tucking me in. I felt small, hollowed out, as if he let go, I'd spin out of control. He slid in next to me, holding me against his side as we listened to the rain.

We never turned the TV on. Just lay there, trading secrets and stealing kisses as the rain danced on the roof above us. For the first time, I didn't feel like I was going to lose myself to please someone else.

***

Cactus

"I know what I saw." Tumbleweed hit the edge of the table with his fist. "Full-face helmet. Dark clothes. It was them."

Tumbleweed had gone out to the nearest gas station early this morning in the rain for more chew. He said he had seen nothing at first, but when he'd left, the gang had surrounded his bike. When he'd made it back to the clubhouse, he'd hollered for Scorpion to call a meeting.

So, Scorpion was listening to Tumbleweed instead of me? Fine. I didn't give a fuck. I'd done my job, but Tumbleweed had been relentless before sunrise. Sending him to voicemail hadn't helped. The bastard had kept calling, one right after another, until I finally picked up.

The executive team had been sitting in our seats for hours. There was no point in going around in circles over the same bullshit if we weren't going to do anything about it. Fuck this. I could have been lying in bed next to Roxy, warm.

"I'm telling you, fuckers. It was them. They boxed in my bike, waiting for me to walk out." Tumbleweed moved the piece of chew in his cheek to the other side, spitting into an empty water bottle.

"It's the closest gas station to the clubhouse. Do you think they were waiting for one of us?" Flash shifted in his seat, writing some notes down for club records none of us would ever see.

"Yes," I answered. "They came for me too, but no one was interested when I tried to warn you. Roxy said they ate lunch at the saloon yesterday." I filled in the details. "They're here, and we're going to be dragged into the middle of a cartel war."

"When did you say something?" Aces looked at Scorpion as they sat at opposite ends of the table.

"You fucking kidding? You were busy playing pool." The mounting danger was inevitable, and we needed to be prepared, but they had been too busy playing with their dicks.

"They were at the saloon?" Scorpion finally said something, and that made me livid all over again. He'd ignored me when I'd called about the hijacked shipment. When I'd walked into the clubhouse to warn him, he'd humiliated some chick. Now, he was concerned. He should have been tearing through every contact we had, pulling favors for information. Fuck.

I said nothing, shooting him a look of my own. I didn't want to fight, but I didn't understand him. He'd worked tirelessly to build the club into what it was today. Our connections, the runs, the club's security were all because of Scorpion. How could he let the club crumble to the ground, nothing more than dust?

"Huck, I want round-the-clock protection on the saloon and the house. Use brothers, not prospects."

His favoritism was showing, and I shook my head. He'd play the devoted father while there was a threat and still screw my sister over emotionally. He was leaving out Roxy, Lulu and Francene. I didn't think any of them were specific targets, but it wouldn't be unreasonable for the gang to think they could intimidate us through the women.

"What about the rest?" I asked.

"Who?" He raised an eyebrow in fake confusion.

I wanted to smash his smug face into the table until his nose broke. "Francene and Jim live out on the ranch. Their nearest neighbor is over five miles away. No one's going to hear them scream. Lulu has her mother and sisters. Roxy's in the motel. They wear fucking name tags. How many Lulus do you think are in a town this size? It's easy to find them."

"No." His voice rang out with finality. I could push, but I wouldn't get anywhere, and no one else was taking a stand. He didn't think they were worth protecting because they weren't Angelica. It was a mistake.

"If we're not doing overnights, maybe we should do pickups. Make sure they get to and from the saloon safely," Eights murmured into the stillness of the room. "I'd volunteer to help if we don't have enough prospects."

"They were coming after us and probably figured we owned the saloon. I doubt the actual waitresses are targets." Scorpion leaned back in his chair.

"The gang could use them to attack us. If something happens to them on our watch, are any of you going to live with yourselves? It will be their blood on our hands." I was hoping the other brothers would back my play, and then Scorpion wouldn't have a choice but to offer them protection.

The room went silent, each man eyeing the person sitting next to him.

"Something else to consider," I continued. "We still have runs to complete. They've tried to hit us in town and in the desert. If the money isn't flowing, and we're under attack, how many of the brothers are going to stick around? Loyalty here is only as good as the pay."

"It wasn't always like that." Aces stared at Scorpion.

"I don't know what you want me to do about it. We needed able bodies, and that's what we got. Their loyalty wasn't in question then." He shifted in his seat. "It's not like we can beat them into submission."

"Why? That's what you do to Angelica." The words were out of my mouth before I even knew I'd said them. It'd been a constant thought lately, and I was curious what his response would be.

Scorpion blinked like I'd sucker-punched him, but I didn't take the bait. I wouldn't need much to explode, my hands already clenched in fists. I was done with words. They no longer worked on him.

My phone rang. Once. Twice. No one said a word as I finally picked up on the third try. "What?"

"Grant, I can't find her."

My back stiffened, a chill creeping down my spine. *We were too late.* "What's going on?"

"Roxy's missing." Angelica took a shaky breath, and I was already out of my seat, heading for the door. "There's a gas leak at the motel. When the kid who works in the office didn't see Roxy, he came running to the saloon. It's the weekend—she's off. People are coughing. Fire and police everywhere, but no Roxy."

"I left her in bed this morning. They searched her room, right?" I didn't bother with my helmet as I started my bike. I didn't want to waste any time.

"The motel is a square, and they started the search on the other side. I've tried to tell them, but no one's listening to me, and the fire marshal isn't here."

It was a ten-minute drive to the motel. I made it there in five. Pulling into the lot, I scanned the faces. There were people everywhere. Some were on the phone, kids were crying, but I couldn't find her. No Roxy. Just sirens, lights, and my pounding chest.

"Oh, thank God, you're here." Angelica rushed over to me, but her eyes went over my shoulder. The executives and a few of the club members had followed me. I hadn't realized it, too concerned with finding my woman.

I'd tried to give her space. Tried to be patient. Fuck that shit. For the first time in my life, I had someone who saw me, all of me, and didn't shy away. She was mine, and I wouldn't lose her. This was Tombstone. If someone touched her, I wouldn't ask questions before I shot first.

Chapter Twenty-Five

Stick the Landing

Cactus

"They're not sending anyone to search her room." Angelica stabbed a finger at Roxy's door. "It's right there."

I tuned her out, focusing only on the room. The police had roped off the motel with yellow caution tape, but that wouldn't hold me back. Planning to jump over it, I ran. However, as I lifted my leg to clear the tape, an officer stepped in front of me. I had to skid to a stop in order to avoid knocking him over.

"No one's allowed beyond the tape." He pointed at me, his cheeks red. He appeared to be Roxy's age, and I wanted to call him son to see if his face would turn as red as a tomato. The kid probably thought the badge gave him swagger, but he hadn't seen enough life to wear it.

"Look, my girl's missing. I'm going to check her room, and you can either come with me or step aside."

The officer unclipped his radio from his belt. "I got a biker making noise. Says there's still a girl in a room on the west side."

"We're doing a grid search now. Tell him to stand down, or he's going to jail. I don't have time to deal with the club," a voice cracked through the radio.

I lunged to shove past the officer, but he held out his hand, forcing me to stop. I didn't dare touch him, afraid he'd arrest me out of spite.

"That's threatening an officer," he said, unclipping his taser from the holster.

I wanted to hit him. One quick shot to the temple to knock his ass out. It'd be worth it, but I'd get cuffed. Roxy was going to need me, and that was the only thought that mattered.

I'd never asked for help, and especially not from the club. I was usually the one they called when shit hit the fan, so when Tumbleweed and Eights boxed the officer in, I stood there staring at them. It wasn't uncommon to trade favors among club members, but I wondered what their endgame was. They'd never come to my defense before, and I didn't trust their motives. Whatever their reasoning, I'd take it for now, but they better not ask me for a thing.

The officer would shift to one side, running into Tumbleweed. He'd try to bypass him, sliding again to the other side, only to be met by Eights. They never touched him, but they kept the officer busy, asking questions. The first one I heard was something about his badge number, like they gave a fuck. I was still standing there, watching them, when Huck grabbed my arm. Together, we jumped the tape.

"You're going to need me to break down the door," he said as we climbed the stairs. Outside her room, he yanked his bandana up over his nose. It was a good thing he was with me because I didn't have any rational thoughts. Following his lead, I was eager to get to her.

Huck was the largest man in the club, so when he raised his boot and hit it against the lock, the door splintered open. "It's a gas leak, so we have to hurry." He moved to the side, letting me enter first.

I dashed through the door, only to stop immediately. She lay unconscious where I had kissed her goodbye merely hours ago. Her face was ghostly white against her black hair. My eyes instantly went to her chest, but I couldn't tell if there was any movement. I wanted to beg her for forgiveness. I'd never leave her again, I told myself as I flew to her side.

Checking her pulse, I felt the weak beats against my fingertips. Relief rushed through me so quickly, my knees almost gave out. She was still alive, and as long as she was breathing, no matter how shallow, she was mine. That was all that mattered. We'd figure out the rest when she was better. "You're not leaving me," I told her, not giving a fuck if Huck heard.

Opening the nightstand drawer, I grabbed her money bag, throwing it at Huck. "Grab her shit. She's done staying here." I ignored him as I slid the covers back. She'd gotten up sometime today, putting on a t-shirt and her sleep shorts. "It's alright, sweetheart. I'm here." Picking her up, I settled her in my arms, but as I pivoted towards the door, I paused.

"Huck!" I screamed, getting his attention. I'd meant for him to shut her suitcase and grab it, but he'd taken me literally, running around for any little thing. "Look!" I tilted my head towards the front wall. I needed another brother to back up my claims when I took them to our executive meeting. After this, the brothers would have no choice but to believe me. They'd left a message painted in red on the wall. "Tick. Tock. The Saints are old news on the block. The clock will strike one when they're done."

I had no clue what it meant, but I didn't have to guess who had sent it. Underneath the words was a painted phoenix, done in reds and oranges. It was the same image I'd seen on the biker's wrists we'd met in the desert. *How long were they in this room with her?*

"Fuck, we need to go." I heard Huck, but my feet were stuck to the ground. There was a whirling sound between my ears, and the only thing I could focus on was the crude painting on the wall.

Anger flashed through me, followed by a mixture of bitterness and shame. I'd told the club this was a possibility, but it'd been too little, too late. They'd already struck, showing they'd used the women against us. The ache in my chest widened. None of it would matter if I lost Roxy. I'd worry about the other women later.

Any of the brothers who still thought we weren't being targeted were sadly mistaken. The bikers had come into the saloon for lunch. They'd been in this room after I'd left this morning. It wasn't hard to imagine they knew Roxy was mine. They'd come after her, sending a message. They were provoking us, forcing us into a war we weren't prepared to fight.

I followed Huck out the door and down the hallway, but he stopped right before the staircase. "They're here," he yelled to the other brothers on the ground floor. "That biker gang. They're watching us." This time, he pointed out to the road that ran behind the motel. There were four bikers sitting on crotch rockets. Black helmets. Black clothes. They were watching us scramble.

"Huck, there's a bomb. That's why they're here. They're here to watch when it explodes. Move." He took the stairs two at a time, but I didn't have that luxury while holding Roxy.

"Fucking dammit. Get those people back. This whole place could blow." Huck was waving his hands in the air, trying to direct the brothers from halfway across the lot.

As my foot hit the last stair, a loud boom sounded from somewhere behind us. Heat tore across my spine, but I kept moving, tucking her closer to my chest. The windows were breaking, glass flying everywhere. "I'm not letting you go," I whispered to her, bending over to shield her. "I'll lose myself if I do."

I heard motorcycles revving, but I didn't pay them any attention as I scanned the crowd, looking for my next move. I was learning they didn't always need me to wipe their asses. The brothers would give chase, hoping it would end in a fight. They could fill me in later when the dust had settled. I'd normally go on a rampage, eliminating the club's enemies, but if the brothers didn't step up, I wasn't sticking my neck out alone.

If we were to have any chance of eliminating them, we needed to learn who their leader was. The bikers were just following orders, but someone wanted credit. The clock was ticking. If the club wanted a war, they'd better be prepared to fight one.

"Sir," a paramedic called out, standing on the other side of the tape. "Over here." He waved his arms around to grab my attention.

The cop yelled something I couldn't process. Voices blurred into static noise. All I saw was the paramedic directing me to lay Roxy on the stretcher. Standing at the back of the ambulance, I watched as one paramedic pulled an oxygen mask over her face, while the other checked her vitals. Her face was blank. No movement. No color. She wasn't invisible, just too quiet. Like she was already gone.

"You might have gotten to her in time. She's breathing on her own, but it's shallow. You the husband?"

"Yeah." I didn't even think twice, even though the thought of marriage scared me shitless. We'd said we'd take this slow, but I wasn't walking away. I'd already given her my soul, and I didn't need a fucking piece of paper to prove my devotion.

"If you want to ride with us, we're leaving in a second for the ER, or you can meet us there."

Angelica's hand on my arm startled me. I'd forgotten she was here in all the chaos. I wrapped my arm around her shoulders, stealing some of her strength. "She needs you, Grant." Ang let out a heavy sigh. "You need her, too. Second chances don't always come. Don't waste this."

***

When they brought Roxy into the ER, everything blurred. Voices clashed. Scrubs ran in and out of her cubicle in bright colors. Machines clicked incessantly, and somewhere an alarm was screaming. My focus narrowed to her, staying as close as I could without getting in the way. I would never forgive myself if I failed to prevent her from suffering something else.

It was over just as fast as it had started. For now, they had averted the crisis. The crowd dispersed, taking the chaos with them. Everyone vanished in a cloud of scrubs, and only silence remained as I sat by her bedside.

"You drive me crazy," I rasped, scared that I'd never hear Roxy respond again. No one had said anything to me about her condition, but I'd heard them speculating from outside the curtain. They spoke in code, the acronyms flying so fast I couldn't keep up. I'd tried to look the shit up on my phone. Nothing matched. Every answer led to more bullshit. Nothing helped.

"Sweetheart, I promise you. I will make them fucking pay for this." My voice cracked halfway through, fear creeping in. The phoenix drawing had sealed their fate. I didn't know who they were yet, or why they had targeted her. When I found out, I'd burn their world down. I wouldn't stop, no matter how many favors I had to call in.

"You've changed me. I thought I'd buried this part of myself, and now, you've made me need you." I didn't know if she could hear me, but I couldn't stop spilling every emotion she'd made me feel. "Losing you would have been a lot easier if I hadn't fallen for you." I swore there was a light pressure, like she was squeezing my fingers. I checked for another sign, hoping to see anything, but there were no other changes.

"I don't know how you'll react when you wake. We won't be one of those couples who can't communicate. Fuck that. I'll tell you everything I can. If it's about you, it's your fucking business. Some shit though will remain hidden. Not because I don't trust you, but for your safety. You'd better be listening because I'm only saying this once." I bent down and kissed the top of her hand. "You haven't brought it up since our first fight, but if you decide to leave, I won't stop you."

I pressed my forehead against the back of her hand. "You'll take everything I am with you. I function only in your world, sweetheart. You're too young for a bastard like me, but I'd stopped giving a fuck long before I changed your tire." I coughed, hiding the lump in my throat. "I've seen you asleep more than awake, but I still can't look away. Even if you don't want me, I'm yours." I brushed my thumb across her knuckles one more time, letting the truths I'd never meant to say linger in the room.

There was a knock on the wall, and I raised my head before the curtain slid back.

"Hello, I'm Dr. Corvin."

My jaw dropped. Standing at the foot of Roxy's bed was Delilah, the woman Scorpion had tried to set me up with for his own personal gain.

"Small world, and seems to get smaller. I split my ER shifts between here and Tucson General." She sat in the other chair next to me. "I understand now." She nodded towards Roxy.

I stared, blinked. Swiping a hand over my face, I hoped I was wrong, but when I opened my eyes, she hadn't moved. "What the fuck were you doing in the clubhouse?"

She laughed, the sound grating on my last nerve. "It keeps me entertained for a while." Delilah shifted in her chair. "I'll understand if you want me to get you someone else. The paramedics said her husband had come with her, but I didn't realize that meant you."

I didn't bother to correct her. If Delilah fucked this up, I'd ruin her life. I wouldn't have to dig deep. The brothers would easily sell her out, not wanting to cross me.

She nodded. "So, her blood work is back, and it's what we suspected. Carbon monoxide poisoning. Odorless. Colorless. She probably didn't know what was happening. Most people feel sick, lie down, and don't wake up."

My grip on Roxy's hand tightened. I needed Delilah to cut through the fucking bullshit and tell me if she'd be alright. "When will she wake?"

"I'm guessing in a few hours. There's no magic drug. All we can do is give her oxygen and wait. You'll see her improving, more color, easier breathing. Give it time." She stood, circling to the front of the bed. Delilah's eyes landed on where I was holding Roxy's hand. "She's lucky," she said, sliding the curtain back and walking out.

I kissed the back of Roxy's hand again. "If you remember any of this, I'll explain. I'll even let you yell at me, but nothing happened. The brothers tried to set me up because you both have raven hair. Delilah's not you. She never could be. I'd already made my choice."

My head tilted back, resting against the wall. Listening to the machines was going to drive me crazy, and I couldn't sit still. I had always been a man of action, and as long as I had a few hours to kill, I'd get things done. Pulling out my phone, a slow grin formed on my lips.

Cactus

She's okay.

Staying at least the night.

I need you to do me a favor.

I detailed everything I needed Angelica to take care of for me. Ang would understand where this was heading, maybe even more than I did. Roxy would never step into the motel again. It was now uninhabitable. She sure as fuck wouldn't live with me in the clubhouse. I wouldn't even bother asking her again.

Ang would come through with the housing, but there was something else I'd need to take Roxy home.

I sent the second text to Aces.

Cactus

Fix the car.

It's time she got her wheels back.

It was her car. Her choice. Still...I'd make damn sure she ended up where she belonged.

Chapter Twenty-Six

Home Is Where Your People Are

Roxy

The machines in my hospital room clicked and beeped, even though I wasn't connected to any of them. It felt like being haunted by someone's ghosts. I ground my teeth, focusing on the pain until each sound was over. I wanted to beat each machine with a baseball bat, watching the pieces fly all over the room, but I'd be bankrupt for a few minutes of fun.

I sat on the edge of the hospital bed, waiting for them to disconnect my IV. If I weren't deathly afraid of blood, I'd pull the needle out myself. The hospital doctor had checked on me over an hour ago. He'd said I was good to go and he'd let the nurse know to prepare for discharge, but here I was, still waiting. As quickly as they wanted to kick me out, they were moving at a snail's pace.

Cactus had said nothing, sitting in the stuffed chair. It looked uncomfortable, but the nurses had told me he hadn't left—not even to get a cup of coffee. They said they had never seen a husband so devoted to his wife. Cactus had restored their faith in love as he talked to me and held my hand.

I had said my piece after he'd barged into my room the night the girls had taken me to the bar. I didn't think things would change, but they had. He'd repeatedly made room for me in his life, reinforcing the truth, and yet, I was still looking for the lies. Some part of me still believed he'd leave. I wasn't worth readjusting his whole life for.

The morning of the gas leak, I'd paced in front of the TV, trying to gather my thoughts. I should have taken the leap of faith, but something held me back. He was exactly who he'd shown me he was, so why was I so conflicted?

I remembered little after that. I'd felt sick to my stomach, thinking I'd eaten something funny. A nap had sounded good, giving whatever it was time to pass. Instead, everything faded to black.

The nurse finally finished up the last few things. She tried to tell me what signs to watch out for, but I only caught half of the shit. I felt fine, and after two days of being stuck in the hospital, I was done with this clusterfuck.

When she mentioned I had to be wheeled out, I lost it. I wasn't waiting around for some volunteer when my legs worked fine. I'd had enough, and I sprinted past her, wanting to go home.

Home?

I'd found my place in Tombstone. Friends I'd consider family, a job I loved, and Cactus. He was the only variable I couldn't predict, and I didn't dare ask. What if he didn't see things the same way?

If he didn't, I would have to leave everything behind. I couldn't stomach staying in a life I couldn't keep. He had the power to destroy me, even though I'd sworn never to allow anyone to hurt me again.

Cactus reached for my hand, interlocking our fingers together as the exit doors opened into the parking lot. "Your chariot is this way."

I believed in soulmates. I shouldn't have, knowing my history, but deep down, I thought there was someone for everyone. You just had to find them. My hand fit Cactus's perfectly, and if that wasn't a sign, I didn't know what was.

He led me past the first couple of rows of vehicles in the hospital's parking lot, but I hadn't seen his bike. It was distinguishable, the paint a desert motif in browns and blues. Past a few more cars, and there it was.

Aces had fixed my car.

He's sending me away. Aces didn't fix things for free. Cactus had to have told him to. My heart sank, and my stomach knotted. It was the last thing I wanted, but I would go if it made his life easier. I wouldn't beg for his attention, and having my car fixed was a sign he didn't want me.

Cactus opened my door, and when I slid into the passenger seat, I instantly looked behind me, hoping my suitcase was in the back seat. I'd have at least a change of clothes, and the suitcase was sentimental. I'd sold everything I owned when I'd left New Jersey, but I had been tired of the plastic bags, buying it with the first tips I'd collected from the saloon. Now, there was nothing, and they had cleaned the car. I couldn't help but feel as if they had wiped my existence away with it.

I didn't have a clue where I was as Cactus drove through neighborhoods I'd never seen. My mouth opened to ask, but I quickly closed it, fearing he wouldn't give me a straight answer. It would just add to my anxiety. At least it didn't look like we were heading to the clubhouse.

He made a right into a place called Sierra, taking the corners as if he'd been there a million times. The houses were cookie-cutter, but I imagined normal stuff. Kids running in the yard, yelling at their friends across the street. The moms sitting on the front porch, gossiping. It didn't help we passed a mother and her young daughter walking out of their front door. That wasn't a life I had wanted for myself, but for a moment, it was a real possibility.

Cactus turned into the driveway of a light gray home. He reached into the cupholder, hitting the button for the garage door. It went up smoothly, but that couldn't be right. He didn't own a home.

Are robbing a house? I was with a man who'd broken into my motel room most days, but I knew him. He didn't need me for something like this. Nor would he ever put me in danger voluntarily. Also, the garage was empty, so he wouldn't find expensive tools, and I'd lend him my car if he really needed one.

"Stay here."

Prick. I smiled on the inside.

He walked around the trunk of my car, whistling. I would have cracked a joke about being able to carry a tune, but none of this was making sense. I should have confronted him, but yelling wouldn't make him talk any faster. He'd hold it in until he was ready, so I remained silent.

Cactus opened my door. "What?" he asked innocently as he unbuckled my seat belt.

"You know I hate surprises. They make me anxious. I don't know what's going on."

"Humor me for a sec. I get only one chance to do this right." He kissed me quickly before picking me up bridal-style.

"Put me down."

"Don't make me flip you over my shoulder." It wasn't a threat. He'd done it before, so I knew it was a promise. I tightened my arms around his neck, closing the space between us. We moved as if we'd done this hundreds of times, not twice.

Cactus opened the door in the garage, stepping through to the house. He sat me on the countertop in the kitchen, bracing his hands against the edge. "Why are you pissy, sweetheart?"

The white wall behind him was as sterile as the hospital had been. The irony hit hard. This didn't feel like a fresh start. I didn't want to be angry with him, but if he was planning on hiding me, I'd rather he'd said goodbye. "I'm confused, and the longer you don't tell me what's going on, the more it makes me think we're over. You're sending me away." I socked his arm. It probably hurt me more than it did him, but he flinched like I'd just clubbed him.

"The motel's gone. They're going to demo it once the fire investigation is done." He genuinely smiled. "If you want, we can live in my room at the clubhouse."

"Fuck, no." That would never happen. I tried to glance around, but his kiss pulled my focus back to him, cutting off whatever fight I had left.

"You need somewhere to call yours. I knew this was for sale." His hands shifted, his knuckles going white as he gripped the counter. "Selfish on my part." He shrugged, lowering his eyes to somewhere around my neck. "I bought it for us, so that you'd have something real. Somewhere you'd want to call home."

"Don't make me beg for affection you're not willing to give," I breathed. I pulled a move from Cactus's playbook. I reached under his beard, found his chin, and pushed up to make him look at me. "Is it? Are you going to stay here? I don't want to stick around, waiting for you to show, husband."

"They told you?" he asked, referring to the nurses.

I made a noncommittal noise. "They gushed about how romantic it was. I almost believed them until I saw my car."

His face shifted, and his eyes narrowed. "Oh fuck. I didn't think how that would look to you. You saw your car and assumed I was going to say goodbye?"

My eyebrows shot up. *What else was I supposed to think*? "You were the one to tell Aces, so I thought you were taking me to the highway. We end up here." I waved my hands around. "I'm not even sure where we are."

"I did. I couldn't put you on the back of my bike after everything. Besides, we're a few more miles from the historical district than you were originally. You're going to need it to go back and forth." He smiled, but his eyes held no emotion. They didn't light up like they normally did when he was excited.

"I told you I was confused. I've gone so long without my car, I assumed it meant you were done with me. Then you pulled up to this house, and I thought you were going to dump me here. Are you seriously going to be here every night?"

"I know you have a hard time with change, but nothing will, except we'll live here. Most nights, I'll be home, all up in your space." He stroked my inner thigh. "Some nights, I'll have to stay in the clubhouse, especially when I'm leaving town." Cactus paused. His jaw clenched as if the words tasted bitter.

"I won't grill you about other women every time you're there." It wasn't my style. If I couldn't trust him not to touch, there was no point in building a life with him. We would have failed from the start.

His eyes blazed, trapping me in his gaze. I couldn't look away for fear I'd miss something. "I need you to know I haven't been with anyone since you showed up in town. Anyone, Roxy. I won't disrespect you like that."

"Why didn't you say something sooner?" I wanted to shake him, as if that would make him talk faster.

"I've walked through hell with less on the line. I don't want you questioning your worth, asking why you weren't good enough to hold my attention. That's a bunch of fucking bullshit, and right now, I want to give you the reassurance I won't stray."

"I love you," I said, loud and clear so that there was no mistake. All the doubt I'd harbored, looking for a reason this wouldn't work, fell like crumbled cinder blocks. I'd rather risk the pain than miss the opportunity to be with him.

"Say it again."

"I love you," I whispered. I wanted it to soak into every inch of him.

"I don't always know how to show you love. Let me prove it to you. For as long as you'll let me."

If I wanted this to progress, I was going to have to be the one to make the first move. I'd spent years worried about pleasing my partners, only now realizing they never cared about satisfying me. Maybe that was why this moment was so important. Every touch, every action said love more than the words ever could.

Leaning forward, I nipped at his lips, waiting until they parted to slide my tongue inside. He said nothing, letting me take control as I reached for the back of his head. I ran my fingers through the short dark hair, scratching at his scalp. He groaned, the sound vibrating down my throat.

I loosened the strap of his belt, tugging it through the buckle. Grasping the zipper of his jeans, I whispered, "I want to christen every room of this house with you, but our first time should be right here."

He shifted, his hand leaving the counter to cover mine. A spike of doubt hit me. *Am I doing something wrong? Why is he stopping me when this is what we both wanted*? I pulled away, not sure what to do.

"Are you sure about this?" he asked, raising his hand to my chin. "I can wait, and the countertop isn't going anywhere."

I didn't want to wait—not when I was this close to finally feeling what it meant to be with someone I loved. I threaded our fingers, guiding his hand away from my face and letting it linger over my inner thigh.

He brushed the skin before sliding his fingers underneath my shorts. "Take them off."

I leaned back on my elbows, hooking my thumbs into my waistband, but I froze. I had experience, but no one had ever looked at me like they could set me on fire. Cactus's eyes burned with the same heat as his touch, and the weight of it gave me pause. A flutter of anticipation twisted low in my stomach.

His hands went back to the counter before he leaned over, his eyes never leaving mine. "You get nervous, we stop. Something doesn't feel right, we stop. There's plenty of time for the rest of our lives." He kissed me once, slowly and surely, before stepping back to give me room to decide.

Nothing changed my love for him, but this was the reassurance I needed. I shifted against the counter, shimmying my shorts and panties down my legs. I tossed them at his chest, but he didn't flinch, letting them drop to the floor between us, eyes still locked on me. He placed his hand flat in the center of my chest, holding me in place.

"Stay there." Cactus lifted my legs and hooked my knees over his arms, holding me open. "Don't look away." He lowered his head, licking directly into me.

I'd never had anyone use their mouth on me before, and I wasn't sure which sensation I was supposed to be paying attention to. His beard scratched my thighs, while his mustache teased my clit. The contrasting sensations made me gasp, my hands digging into his hair to anchor him to me. There was no rhythm to his tongue. He explored me at his own pace, like he had all the time in the world, and I was the best meal he'd ever eaten.

A real groan escaped me. I was so used to fake moaning, the sound surprised me. "Do it again," I demanded, wanting to make sure this wasn't a one-time thing. He didn't stop sucking my clit until more moans poured out of me. When I was close to falling over the edge, he gently bit me. I never knew a little sting of pain could feel like freedom. It did, pulling me apart from the inside out.

I fell backwards, lying on the counter as my elbows gave out. "Don't stop," I begged. "Please, Grant." He licked some more into me, not giving me a break between my first orgasm and the buildup to the second. I wasn't sure I could handle another one, but I didn't want to stop.

This time, he didn't let me fall. Standing over me, he wrapped my legs around his waist. My arousal glistened in his beard. I reached out, curiously running my finger through the damp strands to catch it. Bringing it to my lips, I wanted to know what he made me taste like. Sliding my finger in my mouth, I sucked until it was clean.

He moaned, low and deep. Holding his hand out for mine, he placed my finger on my clit. "Keep this warm for me, sweetheart."

I'd never touched myself before. Not like this. Not with someone watching. Maybe it was strange to admit that, but no one had ever made me feel safe enough to want to. Not until him.

When I didn't instantly move, he guided my finger in small circles until I could move on my own. A hot streak slid through me. I felt like I was burning from the inside as I continued stroking myself, making the same movements over and over to feel it again and again. Somewhere in the haze, I heard his pants hit the floor, but I couldn't stop. I was chasing the high, but it was just out of reach.

"It's alright. Be a good girl and come for me."

It was the praise I needed. I let out a loud moan, letting my body fall.

"What do you want, sweetheart? We can stop, and I'll go take a really long shower, or..."

"You, Grant," I said without hesitation. He held me against him as I sat up, sliding my ass to the edge of the counter. He notched the head of his dick against me, asking me again what I wanted. "To know what it feels like when someone gives as much as they take."

My fingers gripped the back of his neck, nails digging into his skin as he moved within me. My legs tightened around his waist, holding him close. I didn't want to let him go. Our foreheads pressed together, neither of us saying much as peace settled over the kitchen. I breathed him in, hoping he understood what this meant to me.

For the first time, I felt safe. Loved. I let the walls fall without fear of what would happen next.

Grant wouldn't hurt me—and that changed everything.

***

Angelica

I could hear the laughter from the living room as I walked through the front door. My dating life wasn't going well. I'd simply wanted to find someone to connect to, and I'd been hitting the bottom of the barrel each date. I'd been at another disastrous dinner, and their giggles made me smile for the first time this evening.

Roxy had volunteered to hang out with Bri since my brother was staying in the clubhouse for the night. She didn't want to be alone, and I didn't mind. I'd even taken Bri to the grocery store to buy snacks.

"What are you two doing?" I asked, entering the living room. A movie was playing on the TV, but they each sat on one of the sofas, not paying it any attention.

"Mom! Roxy was telling me some of her old waitressing stories. Did you know she worked at the beach?" Bri was sitting cross-legged, clapping her hands as she bounced in excitement.

"I was telling her about the wannabe bodybuilders and their mafia wives." Roxy threw a few kernels of popcorn into her mouth. "How did it go?"

I threw myself onto the nearest overstuffed chair. "He wanted to know how the saloon was so successful, but my favorite was when he asked how much it would take to get you to work for him." My date spent most of the night grilling me about my business, like it was a job interview. If I left the saloon, I'd leave Tombstone altogether.

Roxy thought it over before she threw her head back and laughed. "A million dollars," she said. "You took a chance on me, and I enjoy working in the saloon. If he thinks he can buy me, then he doesn't know me very well."

"I said nothing about you dating my brother. It wasn't my story to tell, so it'll be interesting to see if he actually looks into you."

"I'm sorry it was a waste, Mom. You looked so pretty, and I had a good feeling about this one." Bri yawned before standing up and saying goodnight.

"Is it bad when even your kid knows your love life is shit?" I asked Roxy with a sad smile, my lips barely turning up at the corners.

"She's not a kid. Bri understands more than you think she does." Roxy shrugged, sympathizing with me. "All of us are excited you're trying to fish in a new pond."

"Should you really be giving advice when you fished in the same pond?" I teased.

"I wasn't looking when Grant found me." Her eyes glazed over, and I had to look away.

I wasn't jealous. I was genuinely happy for my brother and Roxy. However, it was hard not to be bitter at Brice. We were supposed to have our happily ever after. He'd promised me the world and had run at the first hint of responsibility. We talked an hour more about nothing, but eventually I said goodnight to Roxy.

Falling asleep, I dreamed of the perfect life. Brice was in our lives because he wanted to be. He was attentive, a good father, and life wasn't so lonely. Even in my dream, I had to keep telling myself it wasn't real.

I didn't like when he didn't show up for Bri, but even I could no longer make excuses about his man-whoring. The club bunnies hung around the saloon just to talk about Brice's dick within earshot. I wanted to tell them I knew what it looked like, what it felt like. They didn't have to tell me.

I wasn't sleeping well. It was so light I might as well have gotten up. It would have been better than rolling side to side, trying to find a good spot to sink into. Maybe that was why I heard the scrape at my bedroom door. I thought little about it. We lived in a safe neighborhood, and my affiliation with the club wasn't well-known outside of club life. Ignoring it, I fluffed my pillow and rolled over.

A hand grasped my throat, pushing me to lie flat. My eyes flew open, but they couldn't adjust fast enough. A biker wearing a full-face helmet had crawled on top of me. I clawed at his arms, but his grip only tightened around my throat. I couldn't breathe.

"Mom!" I heard Bri scream. A feeling of hopelessness came over me. My baby needed me, and I was lying here, accepting an unknown fate.

Renewing my fight, I kicked, punched, anything I could do to gain the upper hand. The biker released me, only to smack his hand across my cheek. I gasped for air, trying to buck him off, but he hit me again.

As he reached for my throat, the sleeve of his black shirt rode up. He had a tattoo of a phoenix on his wrist. The bright reds, oranges, and yellows seared into my memory.

The gun. I owned a gun, and my brother had taught me how to use it. It was in my nightstand. I just had to reach out and grab it.

"Don't touch her!" Even with the bedroom door shut, I heard Roxy clearly.

I flailed for the nightstand, yanked the drawer open, and blindly searched for the cold butt of the gun. I brought it up, hitting the biker with it. It did little, but he loosened his grip on my neck. I tried to get the gun into position, but the biker grabbed for my arm. The gun went off, the sound ringing in my ears. The biker staggered back. His phoenix tattoo flickered into view once more.

"Mom," I heard Bri scream.

It all went silent.

***

Scorpion was once the most feared man in the territory.

He built Tombstone on bare knuckles and blood.

His reputation preceded him—pay before you play.

Now there's a new enemy in town.

Black helmets. Screaming crotch rockets.

Scorpion buried the man he once was.

He let himself get comfortable.

They attacked his woman.

That mistake is going to cost them everything.

Continue the story in

SCORPION'S VENOM

Scan to preorder and access exclusive bonus content.

Continue The Journey

Fall in Love with J's Universe

Every series stands alone, but the characters you love have a habit of showing up where you least expect them.

If you crave danger, devotion, and love that pulls you in and refuses to let go...

MC (Motorcycle Club) Romance

Saint's Outlaws

Broken men who don't deserve redemption—and the women who give it anyway.

Cactus's Prick

Scorpion's Venom

Iron Shield

Leather. Loyalty. Brotherhood.

Love that hurts in all the best ways.

Unveiled Desires

Unveiled Wishes

Unveiled Wounds

Unveiled Transgressions

Mafia Romance

Vows in Violence

Power, obsession, and love that comes with a price.

Bred to Be Owned

Silent Syndicate

Assassin. Secrets.

A man who will burn the world for the one woman he was never meant to have.

Meet Odin (Prequel)

Odin

About the Author

J. Wine writes addictive dark romance where danger and desire collide.

Specializing in Mafia and Motorcycle Club romance, she plunges readers into high-stakes worlds where loyalty and love are pushed to their breaking points. Her alpha heroes are as dangerous as they are devoted, and her fiercely independent heroines navigate shadowed worlds with strength and heart.

Her stories pulse with sizzling chemistry, emotional depth, and love that refuses to play by the rules.

Step into J. Wine's world—where love is never simple, but always worth the risk.

Acknowledgements

T: To the weird kid from 8th grade—You're going to laugh and ask why I didn't write more. How do you thank the most important person in your life? When you figure it out, let me know.

Vicky: Thank you for your unwavering faith in me. Authoring wouldn't be possible without you. Although I could use a few more unhinged comments. We're making progress. Here's to the next one.

The Parental Units: Hi Mom! I know you're proud that I can string a few sentences together, even if you'll never read them. One day I might write something wholesome just for you, but today's not that day. Hi Dad! This is the book you've been waiting for — plenty of blood and guts.

Pappy and Momma Sandy (RIP): My parents have to love me — they don't have to like me — but you took me in and never once questioned the quirks.

Without you, this story would never have come to life, especially the saloon scenes. You might not remember, but I do. They're based on my first trip to Tombstone, when we had lunch sitting just behind Wyatt Earp. Thank you. (Don't worry — I'm taking care of them. May your memory be eternal.)

My ARC Team: Every time you tell me I'm mean—or that I'm teasing you too much—it just raises the stakes. Thank you for pushing me to go harder and deeper with these stories. They wouldn't exist without you. I would have quit a long time ago.

Maile, Terri, Michele, Stephanie, Wasy, and Lindsey—thank you for leading the charge.

Made in the USA
Coppell, TX
06 March 2026

73321828R00114